SOMETHING'S AFOOT

A NEW MURDER MYSTERY MUSICAL

Book, Music and Lyrics by
JAMES McDONALD, DAVID VOS
& ROBERT GERLACH

Additional Music by ED LINDERMAN

S A M U E L   F R E N C H ,   I N C .
45 WEST 25TH STREET   NEW YORK 10010
7623 SUNSET BOULEVARD   HOLLYWOOD 90046
LONDON   *TORONTO*

Amateurs wishing to arrange for the production of SOME-THING'S AFOOT must make application to SAMUEL FRENCH, INC., at 45 West 25th Street, New York, N.Y. 10010, giving the following particulars:

(1) The name of the town and theatre or hall in which it is proposed to give the production.
(2) The maximum seating capacity of the theatre or hall.
(3) Scale of ticket prices.
(4) The number of performances it is intended to give, and the dates thereof.
(5) Indicate whether you will use an orchestration or simply a piano.

Upon receipt of these particulars SAMUEL FRENCH, INC., will quote the terms upon which permission for performances will be granted.

A set of orchestral parts with piano conductor score and principal chorus books will be loaned two months prior to the production ONLY on receipt of the royalty quoted for all performances, the rental fee and a refundable deposit. The deposit will be refunded on the safe return to SAMUEL FRENCH, INC. of all material loaned for the production.

Stock royalty terms and availability quoted on application to SAMUEL FRENCH, INC.

For all other rights than those stipulated above, apply to Paramuse Artists Associates, 1414 Avenue of the Americas, New York, N.Y. 10019.

Printed in U.S.A.

ISBN 0 573 68072 8

SOMETHING'S AFOOT
Book, music and lyrics by
JAMES McDONALD, DAVID VOS
and ROBERT GERLACH
Additional music by ED LINDERMAN

presented by

THE AMERICAN CONSERVATORY THEATRE

Something's Afoot

Book, Music & Lyrics by
JAMES McDONALD,
DAVID VOS & ROBERT GERLACH

Additional Music & Musical Consultation by
ED LINDERMAN

Directed by
TONY TANNER

with

Gary Beach	**Barbara Heuman**
Willard Beckham	**Lu Leonard**
Douglas Broyles	**Pamela Myers**
Darryl Ferrera	**Jack Schmidt**
Gary Gage	**Liz Sheridan**

Scenic Design by	Costumes by	Lighting by
RICHARD SEGER	**WALTER WATSON**	**FRED KOPP**

Musical Direction by
JOHN PRICE

Orchestra:

Larry Epstein, Bass   John Price, Keyboard
Charles Peterson, Woodwinds   John Rae, Percussion

Production Stage Manager
FRED KOPP

SOMETHING'S AFOOT was also produced by the
Goodspeed Opera House, East Haddam, Connecticut.

Marines' Memorial Theatre
San Francisco, Calif.
4

SOMETHING'S AFOOT, book, music and lyrics by James McDonald, David Vos and Robert Gerlach; additional music by Ed Linderman; directed by Tony Tanner; scenery by Richard Seger; lighting by Richard Winkler; costumes by Walter Watson and Clifford Capone; orchestrations by Peter Larson; musical direction by Buster Davis; production stage manager, Robert V. Straus; stage manager, Marilyn Wilt; was presented by Emanuel Azenberg, Dasha Epstein and John Mason Kirby May 27, 1976 at the Lyceum Theatre, N.Y.C.

CAST
(*In order of their appearance*)

LETTIE .... *Neva Small*
    (*the saucy maid*)

FLINT .... *Marc Jordan*
    (*the caretaker*)

CLIVE .... *Sel Vitella*
    (*the butler*)

HOPE LANGDON .... *Barbara Heuman*
    (*the ingenue*)

DR. GRAYBURN .... *Jack Schmidt*
    (*the family doctor*)

NIGEL RANCOUR .... *Gary Beach*
    (*the dissolute nephew*)

LADY GRACE MANLEY-PROWE .... *Liz Sheridan*
    (*the grande-dame*)

COL. GILLWEATHER .... *Gary Gage*
    (*the old army man*)

MISS TWEED .... *Tessie O'Shea*
    (*the tweedy, elderly amateur detective*)

GEOFFREY .... *Willard Beckham*
    (*the juvenile*)

STANDBYS .... *Meg Bussart, Bryan Hull, Lu Leonard, Sal Mistretta*

All the characters are British.

5

THE PLAYING STYLE:

SOMETHING'S AFOOT is a musical spoof of the whodunit genre. All of the characters are British stereotypes: two of them, Lettie and Flint, are Cockney. The situation is farcical, but, because the plot is a murder mystery, the characters should play the play for real. For maximum comic effect, SOMETHING'S AFOOT should not be burlesqued.

THE MUSICAL NUMBERS:

During "A Marvelous Weekend," four hours pass. The sun sets. The house is lighted for evening. The guests change from traveling clothes into dressing gowns, and, for the ending, into evening dress. "Something's Afoot" and "Suspicious" reflect the mystery. "Carry On" is about courage. "I Don't Know Why I Trust You," "The Man With the Ginger Moustache," "The Legal Heir," "You Fell Out of the Sky," and "Dinghy" are 'turns' for the various characters. "I Owe It All" is the big, '11th-hour' number, and "New Day" is a glowing hymn to a future which will never come to pass.

Because SOMETHING'S AFOOT is a mystery, theatre programs should not list who sings the various musical numbers.

MUSICAL NUMBERS

"A Marvelous Weekend"

"Something's Afoot"

"Carry On"

"I Don't Know Why I Trust You (But I Do)"

"The Man With the Ginger Moustache"

"Suspicious"

"The Legal Heir"

"You Fell Out of the Sky"

"Dinghy"

"I Owe It All"

"New Day"

TIME

Late spring, 1935

PLACE

Rancour's Retreat—

The country estate of Lord Dudley Rancour, located on an island in the middle of a lake, somewhere in the English lake district.

SETTING

The entrance hall to Rancour's Retreat—

Not like any entrance hall one has ever seen: a composite room. From this large, two-story room are doorways or hallways leading to the library, the study, the kitchen and the servants' quarters. There is also a large door leading to the outside: the main entrance into the house. There are stairs leading from the room to a landing, onto which the bedrooms and guest rooms open. Doorways to two of these rooms must be visible, the others may be Offstage. All of the essentials in furniture, props and architecture are included in the text of the play.

Something's Afoot

ACT ONE

The Curtain rises, as we hear three clock chimes. Birds are heard chirping outside, in the sunlight. The stage is in semi-darkness. The outside door opens. LETTIE *enters. She takes off her coat, puts down her suitcase, and takes a long look around the room.*

As the lights come up, LETTIE *strikes the dustcover, Stage Left, which covers the desk and desk chair.* FLINT *is asleep under the dustcover.* LETTIE *does not see him until she strikes the dustcover from the pouff, Stage Right.* LETTIE *turns, sees* FLINT, *screams.* FLINT *awakens.* CLIVE *enters from outside.*

CLIVE. Flint!

FLINT. H'lo, Clive.

CLIVE. (*To* LETTIE.) It's only Flint, the caretaker.

LETTIE. How was I to know?

CLIVE. Now that you do, take those cases into the servants' quarters! Flint, this is Lettie, the new maid.

LETTIE. H'lo. (*She exits into Servants' Quarters.*)

FLINT. Pleased to meet *you!* Things are lookin' up around 'ere. Eh, Clive, where's the missus?

CLIVE. My wife passed on last December. Her heart gave out.

FLINT. Aw, Clive . . . I'm going to miss her bubble and squeak.

CLIVE. (*Stiffly.*) Flint. The guests will arrive momentarily and the house is still not ready.

FLINT. Garn, Clive. I been workin' as fast as I can. The upstairs is done.

(LETTIE *enters, with feather duster, dusting the furniture. She passes* FLINT *and* CLIVE. FLINT *pinches her.*)

LETTIE. Ohhhh! Gripper! (*She dusts her way toward the outside doors.*)

CLIVE. (*Sternly, confidentially, to* FLINT.) Watch yourself, Flint. Lettie prefers the well-manicured hand.

FLINT. Garn, Clive, you don't mean the master?

CLIVE. I'm not at liberty to say. (*Car horn.*)

LETTIE. Clive! There's cars comin' across the bridge! (*Music under.*)

CLIVE. It must be the guests! Lettie, those dustcovers! (LETTIE *begins striking dustcovers.*)

FLINT. How many guests will there be?

CLIVE. Six. (*He exits into kitchen.*)

LETTIE. Where do I put these?

(FLINT *shrugs shoulders,* LETTIE *dumps the covers into his arms and* FLINT *dumps them into the closet.* CLIVE *enters with liquor tray from kitchen. He sets tray on liquor cart.*)

CLIVE. The duster! The chair! (*As the doorbell rings,* LETTIE *puts duster in closet. All three are stationed at the door to greet the guests. Doorbell.* CLIVE *opens the door.* HOPE LANG-DON *enters with hat box.*) You must be Miss Langdon.

HOPE. Yes. That's right. (*Singing.*)
OH, WHAT A LOVELY HOUSE!

CLIVE. I'll take your things, Miss.

HOPE. Thank you. (*Moves into room, singing.*)
OH, WHAT A MARVELOUS ATMOSPHERE!

(*Doorbell.* DR. GRAYBURN *enters with golf clubs and doctor's bag.* LETTIE *and* FLINT *exit front door, then return with bags and go upstairs.*)

CLIVE. Dr. Grayburn, how nice to see you.

DR. GRAYBURN. It's nice to see you again, Clive. Has Lord Rancour arrived?

CLIVE. No, sir, we're expecting him shortly. Dr. Grayburn, this is Miss Langdon.

DR. GRAYBURN. Oh, there's another guest?

HOPE. Hello, I'm Hope.

DR. GRAYBURN. Of course you are.

HOPE. (*Singing.*)
OH, WHAT A LOVELY HOUSE IT IS, HOUSE IT IS

DR. GRAYBURN. Yes, it *is*.

(*Doorbell.* NIGEL RANCOUR *enters. He drops his coat and hat into* CLIVE'S *arms and walks into the room.*)

NIGEL. How are you, Clive? Doctor, what are you doing here? Is Uncle Dudley under the weather again?

DR. GRAYBURN. No, Nigel, just a social visit. Miss Langdon, Nigel Rancour.
NIGEL. (*To* HOPE.) I'm the black sheep nephew. Like a drink?
HOPE. No, thanks, it's rather early for me.
NIGEL. I thought I was invited here alone this weekend. (*Crossing to the bar.*)
HOPE. (*Singing.*)
OH, WHAT A LOVELY, LOVELY, LOVELY, LOVELY HOUSE IT *IS*

(*Doorbell.* LADY GRACE MANLEY-PROWE *enters, anxious, a woman with a problem on her mind.*)

LADY MP. Oh! (*She fumbles in her handbag, finds a calling card, hands it.*)
CLIVE. Lady Manley-Prowe.
LADY MP. (*She snatches back her calling card.*) Bonjour! Bonjour! Who are all these people? (*She enters the room, downs* NIGEL's *drink.*) Is Lord Rancour here?
DR. GRAYBURN. He's expected shortly.
LADY MP. I must see him immediately.
HOPE. (*Singing.*)
AREN'T WE LUCKY TO ALL BE HERE?
LADY MP. Yes, I suppose so.

(*Doorbell.* COLONEL GILLWEATHER *enters with shotgun, wearing a pith helmet.*)

CLIVE. (LETTIE *and* FLINT *come down stairs.*) Colonel Gillweather, sir, let me take your pith.
COLONEL. Oh . . . umh . . . umh . . . thank you. How d'you do. How d'you do. Colonel Gillweather here. Pleased to meet you. I didn't know this was to be a *party.*

(*Doorbell.* MISS TWEED *enters with easel and canvas.*)

CLIVE. Mrs. Tweed!
TWEED. Miss Tweed! (TWEED *comes into the room and sings:*)

SONG: A MARVELOUS WEEKEND

SET UP MY EASEL, I FEEL SO INSPIRED.
WHO COULD FEEL TIRED IN THIS ATMOSPHERE?

CAST OFF THE CARES THAT YOU HAVE
    ACQUIRED,
AND PAY HEED WHILE I'M RECITING,
COUNTRY LIFE GIVES AN INVITING
PROMISE OF A MOST EXCITING WEEKEND.
WE'VE BEEN INVITED TO A MARVELOUS
    WEEKEND
A MARVELOUS WEEKEND IN THE COUNTRY AIR.
    ALL.
WE'VE BEEN INVITED TO A MARVELOUS
    WEEKEND,
A MARVELOUS, INVIGORATING,
GLORIOUS AND STIMULATING,
RADIANT, EXHILIRATING WEEKEND!

FAR, FAR AWAY FROM CIVILIZATION,
TRUE RELAXATION IS OUR GOAL.
WE'LL PASS OUR EVENINGS IN POLITE
    CONVERSATION.
AFTER DINNER WE'LL RETIRE FOR A BRANDY
    BY THE FIRE.
WE'LL BE CARELESS THIS ENTIRE WEEKEND!
    COLONEL. I say! Are the squash courts in order? Are the
archery targets set about?
    CLIVE. Yes, Colonel, everything is in readiness.
    DR. GRAYBURN. Good show!
    COLONEL. (*Singing.*)
PUNTING AND HUNTING WILL BE ON THE
    AGENDA.
    DR. GRAYBURN.
NO NEED TO HURRY ON THIS HOLIDAY.
    HOPE.
BIKING AND HIKING WILL MAKE UP THE
    ADDENDA.
    LADY MP.
I RECOMMEND A BIT OF GAY CROQUETING.
    NIGEL.
I RECOMMEND A TANQUERAY . . . TANQUERAY!
    CLIVE, FLINT, and LETTIE.
PUNTING, PAINTING, SWIMMING, ROWING
PUNTING, PAINTING, SWIMMING, ROWING
BIKING, HIKING, DOMINOING
    TWEED and DR. GRAYBURN.
WE HAVE BEEN INVITED FOR THE WEEKEND.

LADY MP and COLONEL.
MARVELOUS, INVIGORATING WEEKEND.
HOPE and NIGEL.
WE'LL BE MERRY THIS ENTIRE WEEKEND.
ALL. (*Everyone excepting* COLONEL, *ascends the stairs and exits.*)
WE'VE BEEN INVITED TO A MARVELOUS WEEKEND.
A MARVELOUS WEEKEND IN THE COUNTRY AIR.
WE'VE BEEN INVITED TO A MARVELOUS WEEKEND,
A MARVELOUS, INVIGORATING,
GLORIOUS AND STIMULATING,
CASUAL, NOT IRRITATING,
CELEBRATING, RUSTICATING . . .
COLONEL. (*Ascending stairs.*)
PUNTING, PAINTING, DOMINOING.
PUNTING, PAINTING, DOMINOING.
HOPE. (*Upstairs. Having examined her room.*)
OH, WHAT A LOVELY ROOM!
COLONEL. (*Upstairs.*) Yes, yes, my dear. Lovely. Everything here is lovely. I remember, now when was it? . . . back in 1919, when we first had the opportunity to, umh, hmmm . . . (*Exits.*)
HOPE.
OH, WHAT A MARVELOUS ATMOSPHERE!
(*Exits.*)
LETTIE and FLINT. (*Enter.*)
AREN'T THEY LUCKY TO ALL BE HERE?
CLIVE. (*Enters.*) Flint! Dispose of the luggage and park the cars. Lettie! There is much to be done. Follow me. (*Descends and exits into kitchen.*)
LETTIE and FLINT. (*Descend.*)
ABSOLUTELY DEVASTING!
OB-VIOUS-LY INEBRIATING!
DEF-NITE-LY SUBORDINATING!
TOTALLY EXASPERATING WEEKEND!
(LETTIE *exits into kitchen.*)
TWEED. (*Enters from her room.*) Hello, there. I don't believe I know your name.
FLINT. Flint, Miss.
TWEED. Flint. Flint. Solid as a rock. Oh, Flint. I do hope to capture the sunset.
FLINT. You don't!
TWEED. I do. But I don't have the proper magenta.
FLINT. You don't?

TWEED. I do. But it's in the wicker in my boot. Could you fetch it?

FLINT. Yes, Miss. (*Exits, saying.*) A magenta in her wicker. (LETTIE *enters.*)

TWEED. Yoo-hoo! You, who?

LETTIE. Lettie, Miss.

TWEED. Lettie. Lettie, might I have a cup of Ovaltine? I'd like to toast the sunset.

LETTIE. Yes, Miss. (*Exits into the kitchen.*)

HOPE. (*Pops her head out to sing.*)

AREN'T WE LUCKY TO ALL BE HERE?
    (*Exits.* TWEED *starts to exit through the wrong door.*)

CLIVE. (*Entering, seeing* TWEED.) Miss Tweed! That is Lord Rancour's room. Yours is there.

TWEED. (*Going to her own door.*) So it is. I'm such a silly! (*Exits.*)

NIGEL. (*Enters.*)

AHHHHHHH! FRESHEN MY GLASS AGAIN, I FEEL
    SO ELATED!
    (*He comes down the stairs, while* CLIVE *pours gin into a glass for him.* NIGEL *takes the drink.*)

AHHHHHHH!
    (*He ascends.*)

LADY MP. (*Enters, dressed in a wrapper. Meeting* NIGEL *at the top of the stairs, she takes his drink and downs it, then sings an even higher.*)

AHHHHHHH! YOU'RE STIMULATED BY THE
    COUNTRY AIR!
(NIGEL *goes down again, to meet* CLIVE, *who refills the glass.* LADY MP *to* CLIVE.) Has Lord Rancour arrived? I must see him the minute he does. (*Exits.*)

LETTIE. (*Enters from the kitchen, carrying Ovaltine in a cup.*) Ovaltine, indeed. (*She starts up the stairs, meeting* NIGEL.)

NIGEL.

THIS IS THE SETTING TO BECOME TETE-
    A-TETED.

LETTIE.

THIS IS THE SETTING FOR A QUIET AFFAIR.
    (*She and* NIGEL *ascend.*)

A QUIET AFFAIR.

CLIVE. Lettie! (NIGEL *slinks off.*)

COLONEL. (*Enters, meeting* LETTIE *at the top of the stairs. He carries a chamber pot.*) I say. What's this?

LETTIE. (*Ascending.*) It's a chamber pot. It's merely for decoration.

COLONEL. (*Noticing the cup and saucer she carries.*) Oh!
Ovaltine! Lord Rancour thinks of everything! (*He gives*
LETTIE *the chamber pot and takes the Ovaltine.*) Oval-tee-ny.
O-val-tee-ny. (*He exits singing.*)

HOPE. (*Enters from her room, in a wrapper, carrying a neck-*
lace.) Lettie, could you clasp me? (FLINT *enters front door*
with wicker.)

LETTIE. Yes, Miss.

(LETTIE *gives* HOPE *the chamber pot to hold.* HOPE *turns to*
    be clasped. LETTIE *does the clasp and immediately heads*
    onward. HOPE, *left with the chamber pot, turns to say*
    "Thanks," but LETTIE *is gone.* FLINT *is now at the top of*
    the stairs, with cases.)

HOPE.
OH, WHAT A LOVELY . . .
(*She realizes she is holding a chamber pot.*) OH! (*She sets the*
chamber pot atop FLINT'S *burden and exits.* LETTIE *closes the*
drapes.)

FLINT. (*Shrugs.*) Oh! (*Exits, into* TWEED'S *room.*)

LETTIE. (*Descending the stairs, sings.*)
OVALTINE AND NECKLACES AND CHAMBER
    POTS AND GIN.
WHEN THEY GO TO BED AT NIGHT, I'LL HAVE
    TO TUCK 'EM IN!
(*Passes* CLIVE, *exits into the kitchen.*)

CLIVE. (*Through the kitchen door.*) Don't boil the con-
somme! (CLIVE *crosses with vase of flowers to small table*
Down Right of library door.)

FLINT. (*Enters from* TWEED'S *room, holding the chamber pot.*
To CLIVE.) She's already got one!

DR. GRAYBURN. (*Enters, to* FLINT.) Excuse me, have you
seen the . . . oh! There it is! (*He grabs the chamber pot*
from FLINT *and exits.*)

FLINT. (*Descending the stairs.*) Paint. In all them cases,
she's got nothin' but paint. No clothes. Just paint. (*The Clock*
begins to strike "seven.")

CLIVE. (*Pointing to a position at the bottom of the stairs.*)
Flint! The lights! (FLINT *switches on the lights. Calling*
through the kitchen door.) Lettie! (FLINT *takes position,*
CLIVE *joins* FLINT, LETTIE *enters, on the run, cap askew and*
takes position with them. CLIVE *to* LETTIE.) Your cap! (FLINT
helps LETTIE *with her cap. Music swells. Guests appear above*
in all their evening finery.)

HOPE. (*Singing, on the gallery.*)
I'VE BROUGHT A SUPER SWIMMING COSTUME.
COLONEL. (*On gallery.*)
I'VE GOT MY CHESS SET FROM BOMBAY.
LADY MP.
MADRIGALS AT TWILIGHT ARE TOMORROW'S
HIGHLIGHT.
NIGEL.
GET THE OARS AND LET'S GO ROWING.
TWEED.
CHOOSE UP SIDES FOR DOMINOING.
DR. GRAYBURN and ALL.
LLOYD'S OF LONDON HAS INSURED . . . THAT . . .
ALL. (*Descend.*)
WE'VE BEEN INVITED TO A MARVELOUS
WEEKEND,
A MARVELOUS WEEKEND IN THE COUNTRY AIR.
WE'VE BEEN INVITED TO A MARVELOUS
WEEKEND,
SOME FOR PUNTING, SOME FOR HIKING,
SOME FOR PAINTING, SOME FOR BIKING.
SOME FOR CARDS AND DOMINOING,
SOME FOR SWIMMING, SOME FOR ROWING.
PUNTING, PAINTING, DOMINOING, BIKING,
HIKING, SWIMMING, ROWING
GUARANTEE US ALL A GLOWING WEEKEND . . .
WEEKEND IN THE COUNTRY AIR!

(CLIVE *exits to* RANCOUR'S *room.* FLINT *and* LETTIE *exit to kitchen.*)

HOPE. (*Having stepped outside for a second, re-enters.*)
B-r-r-r-r. It's getting chilly. Perhaps I should have a wrap.
NIGEL. A drink would warm you up.
HOPE. No, no thank you. And I did so want to see the rose garden by moonlight.
DR. GRAYBURN. You'll get a complete tour of the entire grounds tomorrow, I'm sure. Rancour's Retreat is Lord Rancour's pride and joy.
HOPE. I can well imagine. I've never seen a house this beautiful. I find it all quite enchanting. You see, it's my very first weekend in the country.
TWEED. This is my first weekend here, although it's as if I'd been here many times. Lord Rancour carries photographs of the Estate as some men carry pictures of their children.
HOPE. How sweet.

NIGEL. I myself have never understood his attachment for this old place.

HOPE. I find it quite charming.

LADY MP. And do you find his Lordship charming, also?

HOPE. Actually, I've never met Lord Rancour . . . I . . .

LADY MP. It looks as if you never will. I find his tardiness extremely derriere.

DR. GRAYBURN. Perhaps he intends arriving in the morning.

COLONEL. No . . . no . . . he'll be down presently.

TWEED. Oh, then he has arrived?

COLONEL. Yes, yes . . . soon after I went to my room, I saw his car pull up.

LADY MP. Then I see no reason for dinner to be retard . . . dez.

TWEED. (*Confidentially, to* HOPE.) I hope dinner is a bit late. One should never rush a good sherry. (*She downs sherry and goes for another one.*)

COLONEL. I'd no idea this was to be a party. I'd thought I alone was invited.

DR. GRAYBURN. My invitation mentioned no other guests.

LADY MP. Mine stated clearly that Lord Rancour wished to speak to me privately.

NIGEL. Really? Mine, too.

HOPE. Yes!

TWEED. Well! It seems we've found a most interesting topic for dinner conversation.

CLIVE. (*Appears at the head of the stairs, steps down one step.*) Ladies and Gentlemen, I have some distressing news. (*He steps down one step more.*) A severe electrical storm is rapidly approaching. (*He steps down one step more.*) Should there be a power failure, candles are distributed generously throughout the house. (*He steps down one step more.*) The rising water level of the lake has made the bridge to the mainland impassable. (*He steps down one step more.*) The master will not be dining with you this evening: Lord Rancour is dead. (*He steps down one step more.*) Dinner is served. (*The step on which* CLIVE *is standing immediately blows up, leaving him dead. The Guests momentarily freeze, then:* HOPE *faints into* NIGEL's *arms.* LADY MP *faints into the* COLONEL's *arms.* TWEED *and* DR. GRAYBURN *advance toward the stairs as the two men seek to revive the two women.*)

DR. GRAYBURN. Oh, my God! (*To* TWEED.) Quickly. My bag. It's in the hall closet. (TWEED *quickly gets the bag.*)

TWEED. Have you smelling salts?

DR. GRAYBURN. I'm afraid he's beyond that.

TWEED. For the ladies.

(*The ladies are reviving.* TWEED *administers to them. The*
COLONEL *advances to the foot of the stairs.* LETTIE *and*
FLINT *enter, on the run.* LETTIE *sees the body of* CLIVE,
faints into the arms of the COLONEL.)

COLONEL. Oh . . . oh . . . oh dear . . . oh dear.

FLINT. Garn.

TWEED. Everyone please be calm. (*She goes to* LETTIE *and
the* COLONEL.) I'll take care of her. (TWEED *revives* LETTIE.
NIGEL *advances towards* CLIVE's *body.*)

DR. GRAYBURN. Stand back please.

TWEED. Yes, everyone be seated. Lettie, if you've quite come
to, I believe we could all use a little sherry.

LETTIE. Yes, mum. (*She begins pouring sherry at the bar.*)

TWEED. Is it as I expected?

DR. GRAYBURN. What did you expect?

TWEED. He is dead?

DR. GRAYBURN. Quite.

TWEED. Lightning, I suppose.

DR. GRAYBURN. No. Someone has tampered with this stair.

NIGEL. You're not trying to tell us it's . . .

DR. GRAYBURN. I'm afraid it is.

TWEED. Intentional.

COLONEL. But . . . but . . . but . . . how?

TWEED. (*Sniffs the air.*) An explosive. The type is yet un-
certain.

FLINT. A bloomin' booby-trap?

DR. GRAYBURN. Precisely.

FLINT. But why Clive?

HOPE. It needn't have been he. It could have been any one
of us.

TWEED. That's true, my dear. Unless . . . unless the device
was carefully controlled.

COLONEL. But . . . but . . . that would be murder! (*Thunder. Lightning. Wind. Rain. A huge storm hits. Everyone sits
on the pouff while* TWEED *sings.*)

SONG: SOMETHING'S AFOOT

TWEED.
SOMETHING'S AFOOT!
AND THE BUTLER DIDN'T DO IT!
OTHERS.
THE BUTLER DIDN'T DO IT?!?!?!?!?
TWEED.
SOMETHING'S AFOOT, AND

IF HE DIDN'T DO IT,
SOMEONE ELSE HAS HAD TO DO IT.
A STORM IS HERE,
WE'RE SURROUNDED BY A LAKE.
   LETTIE.
THE HOUSE IS DREARY.
   LETTIE and OTHERS.
THE WEEKEND IS A BIG MISTAKE.
   TWEED.
SOMETHING'S AFOOT . . . A
SOMETHING VERY SCARY.
(*Spoken.*) Lettie, please, another sherry.
SOMETHING IS QUITE AMISS.
   ALL. (*Except* TWEED, *spoken.*) But the butler didn't do it.
(*Repeated four times, rapidly.*)
   TWEED.
THOUGH I'M NOT BOUND BY SUPERSTITION,
 I'M FORCED TO ADMIT THE SUPPOSITION,
WITHOUT A QUIZ
THAT SOMETHING IS A . . .
   OTHERS. (*While* OTHERS *sing and pour sherry,* TWEED *examines the stairs and re-latches the broken railing.*)
WHAT SAY A LITTLE SPOT OF SHERRY?
WHAT SAY A LITTLE BIT OF SONG?
WHEN ONE HAS A LITTLE SPOT OF SHERRY,
WHAT CAN POSSIBLY GO WRONG?
IN A MOMENT OF UNPLEASANTNESS,
WE NEVER SHOULD PURSUE IT.
   COLONEL.
WHAT HO!
   DR. GRAYBURN.
RIGHT-O!
   NIGEL.
NOT A WHIT!
   OTHERS.
FOR WE'RE QUITE PROTECTED BY THE ONE
WHO KNOWS JUST HOW TO DO IT.
   TWEED. (*Spoken.*) Cheers.
   OTHERS.
SO YOU'LL NEVER FIND US IN AN AGITATING
   SNIT.
HERE'S TO ANOTHER SPOT OF SHERRY,
RAISING OUR GLASSES IN A SONG.
WHEN ONE HAS ANOTHER SPOT OF SHERRY,
NOTHING IN THE WORLD,
IN THE WHOLE UNITED KINGDOM,

NOTHING IN THE WORLD COULD BE WRONG!
COULD BE . . . WRONG
> (*They notice the body.*)

SOMETHING'S AFOOT!
AND THE BUTLER DIDN'T DO IT!
HOW COULD THE BUTLER DO IT?
SOMETHING IS QUITE AMISS.
> TWEED.

DON'T BE BOUND BY SUPERSTITION,
> OTHERS.

THOUGH FORCED TO ADMIT THE SUPPOSITION,
> OTHERS.

WITHOUT A QUIZ, THAT SOMETHING IS A . . .
> TWEED. (*Spoken.*)

Exploding stairs are rather rare,
You just don't find them everywhere.
> OTHERS.

WITHOUT A QUIZ, THAT SOMETHING IS A . . .
> TWEED. (*Spoken.*)

Considering the way he died . . .
I don't think it was suicide.
> OTHERS.

WITHOUT A QUIZ, THAT SOMETHING IS A . . .
> (*Spoken.*)

The situation's not the best
For someone who is a weekend guest.
> OTHERS.

WITHOUT A QUIZ, THAT SOMETHING IS A . . .
> FOOT!
> TWEED. (*Spoken.*)

And the butler didn't do it!
Murder! A very serious business.

FLINT. Garn. A murder. At Rancour's Retreat.

TWEED. Perhaps two.

NIGEL. What do you mean?

TWEED. Recall Clive's last words.

COLONEL. Dinner is served?

HOPE. Lord Rancour is dead! (*All gasp, then advance toward the stairs.*)

TWEED. Stop! The stairs are now safe. Doctor, you see to Lord Rancour. I think it best we remain all together. (DR. GRAYBURN *hurries up to the stairs and off.*)

NIGEL. But what if he needs help?

TWEED. He knows his business. We can better use you down here. Since we'll be spending some time here, I think it best to remove Clive to another room.

LADY MP. I shan't be spending time here. I'm leaving.

HOPE. You can't leave. None of us can leave. Clive said the bridge is impassable.

LADY MP. But we've only the word of a dead man for that. Send someone to make certain.

TWEED. We will do that. But, with order. First, we'll remove Clive. Master Nigel, please assist Flint in removing Clive to . . . the library. (FLINT *and* NIGEL *take up the corpse and exit.*)

LETTIE. (*Unearnestly.*) Is there anything I can do to help?

TWEED. Keep the sherry glasses filled, my dear. And take a bit for yourself. 'Twill sooth the nerves.

LETTIE. That's what I need, all right.

COLONEL. I believe I could do with something a . . . a bit stiffer.

TWEED. Good idea, Colonel; you will have to lead the scouting party to survey the bridge.

COLONEL. A scouting party? By Jove, I haven't led a scouting party since I fought against the Fuzzy-Wuzzies.

TWEED. Yes, Colonel Gillweather.

COLONEL. Should I set off now?

TWEED. No. No, wait until we know Lord Rancour's condition. (FLINT *and* NIGEL *re-enter.*)

COLONEL. (DR. GRAYBURN *enters from* LORD RANCOUR'S *room.*) As you say. By Jove, I should have had you in Inja. With your head and my heart, those Fuzzy-Wuzzies would have ended up . . .

DR. GRAYBURN. (*At the head of the stairs.*) Dead. Lord Rancour is quite dead. (TWEED *rushes up the stairs.*)

NIGEL. But, how?

LADY MP. His heart!

NIGEL. He had a bad heart.

HOPE. It was a *heart* attack!

DR. GRAYBURN. (*To* TWEED, *on the landing.*) It was a *revolver*. Discharged at close range.

TWEED. I trust you didn't touch the revolver.

DR. GRAYBURN. Certainly not. There was no revolver to touch.

TWEED. I see! (*She exits into* LORD'S RANCOUR'S *room.* DR. GRAYBURN *descends stairs.*)

FLINT. The master. Murdered.

NIGEL. Dr. Grayburn. How long would you say my uncle has been dead?

DR. GRAYBURN. It's difficult to tell, three hours . . . probably less.

HOPE. Three hours! That means he was shot while we were in the house!

COLONEL. Ridiculous!

LADY MP. I agree, I heard no gunshots.

FLINT. It's an old house. The walls are thick . . .

TWEED. (*Appears on landing.*) And . . . the revolver was muffled! (*She descends the stairs.*)

DR. GRAYBURN. Most likely.

NIGEL. But who would have wanted to kill my uncle? (*Everyone turns and cocks an eye at* NIGEL.)

TWEED. A murderer, good or bad, usually has a motive.

NIGEL. Quite true, and what would this motive be?

TWEED. I've always been partial to revenge, passion, lust and greed.

DR. GRAYBURN. Recently, on my visits to Lord Rancour, I have noticed an inexplicably tense atmosphere between him and one of his servants . . . Clive!

NIGEL. Right, Doctor! Clive was completely devoted to my uncle, until . . .

DR. GRAYBURN. Until Clive's wife passed away.

FLINT. 'Ere now, Clivé always said that his missus was bein' worked to hard.

HOPE. Then the motive was revenge?

LETTIE. I for one don't think he done it.

TWEED. I don't think he done . . . did it either, my dear.

LADY MP. And why not?

TWEED. Because Clive has also been the victim of foul play.

COLONEL. And . . . and that murderer is probably, say, miles from here by now.

TWEED. Unless . . . he found the bridge impassable.

HOPE. That would mean the murderer is still on the island!

TWEED. Or . . . in this house! (*Everyone freeze and step back—strum on piano strings.*)

DR. GRAYBURN. Then I think we should brave the storm and find out.

TWEED. Just what I had planned. Colonel Gillweather . . .

COLONEL. What . . . what? Oh, time for that scouting party? Let's go, men . . . up and at 'em. Ummmh . . . Flint, we'll need raingear.

FLINT. Aye, aye. (*He takes raingear for the men from the closet. During the* COLONEL'S *speech, the men put on slickers and rain hats, get lanterns from* LETTIE, *and exit.*)

COLONEL. (LETTIE *exits to kitchen and returns with lanterns.*) And lanterns . . . yes. Doctor, you and young Nigel here, take the road to the bridge and survey the battlements there. Flint, you'll be my aide-de-camp. We'll make a wide sweep of the island and rout the enemy from his entrenchment. Then we'll all reconnoiter at the iron gates. You've got your orders . . . into the fray! (*All men exit except* COLONEL.)

COLONEL. (*Walks to the door, turns to the ladies, saluting.*) Don't give up the sh . . . chalet! (*He exits.*)

LETTIE. (*Closes the door behind them.*) They didn't wear rubbers. They'll muck up the carpet when they come back.

LADY MP. *If* they come back. (*The ladies are left alone in the house. Thunder booms. Lightning flashes. The ladies all huddle around the pouff.*) I'm hungry.

LETTIE. Dinner's cold. And what ain't cold's burnt.

TWEED. But, Lettie, do you suppose we could have some biscuits with our sherry?

LETTIE. Yes, mum. (*She starts for the kitchen. She opens the kitchen door, but does not exit . . . lost in thought . . . she is frightened.*)

LADY MP. Well, Miss?

LETTIE. I'm afraid to go in there.

HOPE. (*Puts her arm around LETTIE's shoulder.*) I'll go with you. (LETTIE *smiles weakly. They exit.*)

TWEED. Be careful, girls.

LADY MP. I'm terribly frightened.

TWEED. Nonsense.

LADY MP. The gentlemen left us completely unprotected.

TWEED. We'll make do.

LADY MP. But I'm a mere woman.

TWEED. Poo . . . Poo.

SONG: CARRY ON

FRANKLIN DELANO ROOSEVELT,
WHO RULES THE COLONIES,
SAID, "THERE'S NOTHING TO FEAR BUT FEAR
    ITSELF"
MOST APROPOS WORDS ARE THESE.

THOUGH WE'RE WOMEN THAT IS CLEAR,
WE WILL SOMEHOW PERSEVERE,
PAYING HEED, THOUGH WE'RE DISTRAUGHT,
TO MR. ROOSEVELT'S THOUGHT . . .

DON'T BE AFRAID
WHEN YOU CAN BE COURAGEOUS.
WHY BE AFRAID?
HIGH SPIRITS ARE CONTAGIOUS.
CARRY ON . . .

DON'T BE AFRAID.
THERE IS NO NEED TO COWER.
WHY BE AFRAID?

IT'S NOT OUR DARKEST HOUR.
CARRY ON!

WHEN THE DAY IS BLEAK,
AND YOUR KNEES ARE WEAK,
TELL YOUR FEARS, "AWAY, BEGONE!"
POO, POO! PIP, PIP!
STIFF UPPER LIP.
CARRY ON.

DO NOT CONDONE
EMOTIONS THAT ARE SKITTISH.
YOU'RE NOT ALONE.
REMEMBER WE ARE BRITISH.
CARRY ON!
    (*Spoken.*)
Lady Grace!
    TWEED and LADY MP.
CARRY ON!!
    TWEED. (*Spoken.*) These spears should do nicely. (*She takes down spears from wall over desk.*)
    LADY MP. You expect me to use that?
    TWEED. Of course, my dear.
    LADY MP. Miss Tweed, that's all well and good, but you see . . . (*Sings.*)
I CANNOT APPEAR TO HIDE MY FEAR
FOR I ADMIT TO HAVING QUALMS.
WHEN THE MOMENT'S TENSE, I'VE NO DEFENSE,
JUST PERSPIRATING PALMS.
    TWEED. (*Spoken. Slaps a spear into her hand.*) Rubbish! (*Sung.*)
DO NOT CONDONE
EMOTIONS THAT ARE SKITTISH.
YOU'RE NOT ALONE.
REMEMBER WE ARE BRITISH.
CARRY ON . . .
    TWEED and LADY MP.
CARRY . . .
    LADY MP.
NEVER WEAR A FROWN WHEN YOU'RE FEELING
    DOWN.
AFTER NIGHT MUST COME THE DAWN.
WHERE THERE'S HOPE THERE'S LIFE,
SO FORGET YOUR STRIFE,
AND REMEMBER CARRY ON.
    TWEED and LADY MP.
DON'T BE AFRAID,

WHEN YOU CAN BE COURAGEOUS.
WHY BE AFRAID,
HIGH SPIRITS ARE CONTAGIOUS.
CARRY ON,
CARRY ON!!
   TWEED.
ARE YOUR TENSIONS TAUT?
ARE YOUR NERVES DISTRAUGHT?
ARE YOU LOOKING PALE AND WAN?
   LADY MP. (LETTIE *enters.* TWEED *throws her a spear, then
gets another from the wall.*)
RAISE THE COURAGE CUP,
KEEP YOUR PECKER UP . . .
   LETTIE.
AND REMEMBER CARRY ON!
I'M NOT AFRAID, YOU'LL NEVER SEE ME COWER.
WHY BE AFRAID? OH, NO, I'M RIGHT, DON'T
      COWER.
WHY BE AFRAID? IT'S NOT OUR DARKEST HOUR.
CARRY, CARRY, WE SHALL CARRY ON.
   TWEED and LADY MP. (*Sing with* LETTIE, *as she sings above
verse.*)
DON'T BE AFRAID, THERE IS NO NEED TO
      COWER.
WHY BE AFRAID? IT'S NOT OUR DARKEST HOUR.
CARRY, CARRY, WE SHALL CARRY ON.
   HOPE. (*She enters from kitchen. She gets a spear from the
wall.*)
NEVER WEAR A FROWN WHEN YOU'RE FEELING
      DOWN,
AFTER NIGHT MUST COME THE DAWN.
POO, POO! PIP, PIP!
STIFF UPPER LIP
AND REMEMBER QUEEN VICTORIA!
   ALL. (HOPE *sings the obligatto.*)
DO NOT CONDONE
EMOTIONS THAT ARE SKITTISH.
YOU'RE NOT ALONE.
REMEMBER WE ARE BRITISH.
CA . . . RRY . . .
   LETTIE and HOPE. (*Spoken.*) Our hearts shall burst with
pride!
   LADY MP and TWEED. Forever side by side!
   ALL. O-o-o-o-n. (*Kick line.*)
DON'T BE AFRAID,
WHEN YOU CAN BE COURAGEOUS.

WHY BE AFRAID,
HIGH SPIRITS ARE CONTAGIOUS.
CARRY
CARRY ON!
TWEED. Atten-hut!

(*After the end of the song, thunder booms, lightning flashes, the door flies open and we see* GEOFFREY. *He is dressed in rowing togs, with a pack on his back. Across his chest is the letter "W." The girls drop their spears and run for cover.*)

GEOFFREY. Drat! My letter's running! (*Looking at his T-shirt.*)

TWEED. (*Picks up spear and advances.*) Returning to the scene of the crime, eh?

GEOFFREY. I beg . . .

TWEED. (*To the others.*) They always do that, you know. Advance, villain. (LADY MP *picks up the other spear and* TWEED *nudges* GEOFFREY *from behind.*)

GEOFFREY. I say.

HOPE. The poor fellow is wringing wet. He'll catch his death.

GEOFFREY. An angel of mercy. (LETTIE *closes door.*)

TWEED. He'll catch more than that when we turn him over to the authorities.

GEOFFREY. I'm a bit confused.

LADY MP. Hmmmmff. Well, we're not. We've been much too clever for you.

GEOFFREY. You don't seem to understand.

TWEED. (*She pushes* GEOFFREY *into the desk chair.*) Quiet, harbinger of evil. Lettie, bind his hands and feet. (*She undoes her muffler from round her neck.*)

LETTIE. By myself? I'd rather not, Miss.

TWEED. Lady Grace, I have him covered. Assist Lettie, if you will. (*They start for* GEOFFREY. *He moves back in the chair.* TWEED *menacing with her spear.*) Hold 'fast, varlet. (LETTIE *and* LADY MP *bind his hands and feet with* TWEED'S *rather long muffler.*)

GEOFFREY. I think it possible you have me confused with someone else.

TWEED. I said quiet. We know more about you than you think. We need hear none of your cunning lies.

GEOFFREY. (*To* HOPE.) Gentle miss, I appeal to you.

HOPE. Yes! Yes?

GEOFFREY. Can you do nothing?

HOPE. (*To* LETTIE *and* LADY MP.) Don't cut off his circulation. (*She and* GEOFFREY *smile at each other.*)

GEOFFREY. Thank you.

TWEED. Don't be taken in by his wiles, my dear. The hardest criminal can, on occasion, display charm. (*Offstage, Voices are heard.*)

HOPE. But, Miss Tweed . . .

TWEED. Lettie, I think I hear the men without. (LETTIE *goes to the door. The door swings open.* FLINT *starts to enter the room.*)

LETTIE. Don't muck up the carpet!

FLINT. (*Wiping his feet before entering.*) We've covered every inch of the island.

DR. GRAYBURN. (*Wiping his feet.*) The rising waters have washed out the bridge completely.

COLONEL. (*Wiping his feet.*) We found not a trace of the enemy.

(NIGEL *enters. During the entrances,* FLINT *takes the McIntoshes and lanterns and deposits them in the closet.*)

DR. GRAYBURN. (*To* TWEED.) The murderer seems to have vanished into thin air.

TWEED. Only to reappear (TWEED *reveals* GEOFFREY. *Much murmurs and exclamations.*)

COLONEL. Who is this?

TWEED. If my deductions are correct, this is our man.

NIGEL. (*Amused.*) So this is our murderer.

GEOFFREY. Murderer? Is that what . . . Murderer???

HOPE. Please don't say anything else.

NIGEL. But what would be his motive?

TWEED. Simple. He has a letter on his chest. He is a college student. College students are notoriously impoverished. He came here, hoping to steal something of value, was discovered by Lord Rancour, and promptly did him in.

HOPE. But what about . . . ?

TWEED. One moment, my dear. I haven't finished. Therefore, I deduce that this young man is not only a college student and a thief but our murderer as well. Lettie, if you will check his knapsack, I believe you will discover the weapon. (LETTIE *advances cautiously to* GEOFFREY *and opens the knapsack.*)

LETTIE. . . . a shirt . . . a pair of trousers . . . a cucumber sandwich . . .

LADY MP. Oh, Lettie . . . thank you. (LADY MP *signals to* LETTIE, *who hands her the sandwich. She begins nibbling on the sandwich.*)

LETTIE. There's nothing else in here but . . . (*She pulls out a gun and drops it on floor. Everyone gasps.*)

TWEED. Mustn't smudge the fingerprints. (*She picks up the gun with the point of her handkerchief.*)

DR. GRAYBURN. Miss Tweed, you are remarkable.

COLONEL. Well done. Yes, yes, well done.

GEOFFREY. May I speak?

HOPE. Yes, it's only fair.

TWEED. You may speak. But don't expect us to believe a word you say. (*While GEOFFREY speaks, TWEED goes to the liquor cart, and, with her back to the audience, switches guns for one loaded with a blank.*)

GEOFFREY. Your first deduction was correct: I am a college student. But I'm not a thief . . . I'm a third oarsman. My team and I were rowing on the lake when the storm overcame us. Our tiny craft capsized. The others swam to the mainland, but I, not wanting to ruin my jersey, swam here. It was closer. My intention was to walk across the bridge to the mainland. But, finding it washed out, I came here for refuge.

LADY MP. A likely story.

HOPE. It sounds plausible. (*She and GEOFFREY smile at each other.*)

GEOFFREY. Instead of refuge, I find myself accused of murder . . . a murder I did not commit.

FLINT. There have been two murders.

HOPE. That's right! What about Clive's murder, Miss Tweed? A happenstance thief wouldn't have had the time to wire the stairs.

COLONEL. By Jove, she's right. Good thinking, Miss.

LETTIE. But what about the gun? He did have a gun.

TWEED. (*Takes the gun out of her pocket and sniffs.*) And it has been fired recently.

NIGEL. (*Takes the gun, sniffs.*) Yes, it has.

GEOFFREY. That's our starting pistol. It fires blanks.

NIGEL. In that case, you wouldn't mind my pointing it at you.

GEOFFREY. (*Nervously.*) Why, no.

NIGEL. Then why are you so nervous?

GEOFFREY. It's only that I've never had a gun pointed at me before. (*Everyone else draws back.* HOPE *has a hand to her mouth, another to her breast.*)

NIGEL. And you still maintain that this is a blank pistol?

GEOFFREY. Yes, yes it is.

NIGEL. Well, in that case, you won't mind my firing it at you? (*He fires.* HOPE *screams.* LETTIE *faints into the arms of the* COLONEL. *There is a moment of strained silence.*)

GEOFFREY. I think you can untie me now.

TWEED. Well, well, we all make mistakes. (*She unties him,*

rewraps the muffler around her neck. LETTIE *revives.* FLINT *collects the spears and exits.*)

GEOFFREY. I realize that I'm an outsider, but now that I'm inside, will someone please explain what has been going on?

HOPE. Well, you see . . .

TWEED. I think I'd best explain, my dear. We are all week-end guests of the late Lord Rancour.

GEOFFREY. How late?

TWEED. Approximately three hours and thirty minutes. He and his butler, Clive, have been murdered. This evening.

GEOFFREY. Murdered? Here in the house?

TWEED. Yes. One upstairs. One on. And, naturally, you, being the only stranger in our midst . . . we suspected you.

GEOFFREY. Is help on the way?

COLONEL. How could help be on the way? The bridge is washed out.

GEOFFREY. Have you telephoned? (*There is a moment of silence, as they look at one another.*)

DR. GRAYBURN. Telephone? Of course!

HOPE. Isn't he wonderful?

DR. GRAYBURN. (*Rushes to the telephone on the desk.*) Are you there? Operator? Operator?

TWEED. Dr. Grayburn . . .

DR. GRAYBURN. Are you there? I say . . . (*He continues saying "Hello."*)

TWEED. Dr. Grayburn. I said, Dr. Grayburn, the wire has been cut.

DR. GRAYBURN. Good God, the wire has been cut! Operator, the wire's been cut!

FLINT. (*Enters.*) Anyone seen my garden shears?

TWEED. Hmmmmmmmm. Cut wire. Missing shears.

DR. GRAYBURN. Is this the only telephone in the house?

LETTIE. Oh, no. There's one in every room.

DR. GRAYBURN. Would you check them?

LETTIE. (*Eyeing* NIGEL.) Alone?

GEOFFREY. I'll help you.

HOPE. Hadn't you better change first? You're soaked to the skin.

GEOFFREY. How thoughtful of you to notice. (*He exits up the stairs with his knapsack, following* LETTIE.)

LADY MP. I hope at least one of the telephones is "en service." I don't see how I can stay another minute on this island.

NIGEL. We're all most anxious to leave, Lady Grace.

HOPE. Something has been troubling me.

DR. GRAYBURN. What's that, my dear?

HOPE. You said that Lord Rancour has been dead for approximately three hours.

DR. GRAYBURN. That is correct.

HOPE. Did it happen in his room?

DR. GRAYBURN. I'd say so, yes.

HOPE. Yet, the Colonel saw his car pull up.

COLONEL. I did . . . I did . . . no more than two hours ago.

HOPE. You see . . . that's what has been troubling me.

FLINT. But I drove the Master's car up.

TWEED. You drove the car here?

FLINT. Yes, Miss.

TWEED. And your missing shears most likely cut our only means of communication.

FLINT. My shears must have been stolen. The rest is simple.

TWEED. Nothing is simple when murder is involved . . . Why were you driving Lord Rancour's car?

FLINT. I found it parked beside the west wing. I drove it 'round to the garage, that's all.

TWEED. Did you see Lord Rancour?

FLINT. No. I figgered he'd already arrived and gone straight to his rooms.

TWEED. Perhaps . . . But how do you explain why . . .

LETTIE. (*Appears at the top of the stairs, carrying as many telephones as is humanly possible.*) All the wires have been cut off! (*She brings the telephones down the stairs and deposits them in a heap on the floor.*)

NIGEL. Then we really are completely cut off from the outside world. All alone here on this damned island. (*Everyone sits.* FLINT, *not seeing* TWEED *in the desk chair, starts to sit, then jumps away.*)

COLONEL. I say, anyone up to a romping game of chess?

(*Telephone rings a double "English" ring and continues while everyone frantically scrambles with the phones, trying to get an answer. Then, the ringing stops. Silence.*)

HOPE. There was a ring, wasn't there?

LETTIE. I heard it too.

NIGEL. But that's impossible!

TWEED. The other day, I was reading a treatise on mass hallucination . . .

(*Phone.* GEOFFREY *enters. Phone keeps ringing, while they once again try the instruments on the floor.* DR. GRAYBURN *goes to desk. He finds hidden phone. He says "shush" to everyone. He lifts receiver and says.*)

DR. GRAYBURN. Hello, there. (*POOF! Pink dust emits from the telephone and gasses him to death.*)

COLONEL. Gas!!!

TWEED. Quickly, cover your faces. (*They do.*)

COLONEL. No need for that. The danger lies only with the person in the direct line of fire.

TWEED. Lettie, fetch me the Doctor's bag. I see you know your gasses, Colonel.

COLONEL. I should. Fought in the Great War, you know. (LETTIE *hands the bag to* TWEED, *who takes out stethoscope and listens to* DR. GRAYBURN'S *heart.*)

LADY MP. Quelle fromage!

NIGEL. Is it lethal, Colonel?

COLONEL. Yes, yes. I would say death would be almost . . .

TWEED. (*Looks up.*) Instantaneous.

FLINT. Garn. The doctor murdered, too.

HOPE. Is it murder this time?

GEOFF. It looks that way.

TWEED. Another fiendishly concocted device. A timing mechanism, set to simulate the ringing of a telephone bell.

LETTIE. I thought it sounded like a telephone bell, myself.

LADY MP. What will we do? Quelle catastroph . . . catastroph . . . oh, ph . . . What will we do?

TWEED. First we will remove the body. Master Nigel, if you will, please help Flint remove the good doctor to the library.

(FLINT *and* NIGEL *pick up the body and carry it out, passing the others on their way out.*)

COLONEL. This perhaps is not the time to bring this up . . . but we men have been out battling the elements, and I, for one, could use a bracer of tea.

TWEED. After this harrowing experience, I believe we could all use some tea. Lettie.

LETTIE. I told you, I'm not going in there alone.

TWEED. (*Laughs.*) We'll be happy to accompany you, won't we, Colonel? (LETTIE *has been picking up the telephone instruments.* TWEED *and the* COLONEL *assist her and all walk off toward the kitchen, laden with telephones.* TWEED *looks back.*) Lady Grace?

LADY MP. What? No, no thank you, Miss Tweed. I am très fatigué. If you'll excuse me, I'll go up to my room and lie down for a while.

TWEED. (*As she exits.*) You won't forget to bolt the door, dear?

LADY MP. (*To* GEOFFREY *and* HOPE, *as she starts up the*

stairs.) Forget to bolt the door? (*Music under.*) I'll bolt the door. The windows, too. If you want me, I'll be under the bed. (*She exits.*)

GEOFFREY. One would almost think they'd left us alone for a purpose.

HOPE. Perhaps so I could get to know you better. I don't know you at all, and, yet, I feel I've known you all my life.

GEOFFREY. Me too. You aren't frightened of me?

HOPE. Oh, no, how could I be frightened of you?

SONG: I DON'T KNOW WHY I TRUST YOU
(BUT I DO)

THERE'S A HINT OF HIDDEN DANGER
WHEN YOU MEET A DASHING STRANGER
AND I DON'T KNOW WHY I TRUST YOU
BUT I DO (YES I DO).

FROM THE MOMENT OF OUR MEETING
I FELT WE WERE REPEATING
AN ENCOUNTER WE'D ENCOUNTERED ONCE
BEFORE.

YOU'VE GIVEN MY HEART A LIFT.
YOU'VE MASTERED THAT ANCIENT GIFT. (WHAT
A GIFT.)

YOU'RE A KNIGHT WITHOUT HIS ARMOR,
BUT YOU'RE STILL A PRINCELY CHARMER,
LIKE A LANCELOT, YOU'RE TOO GOOD TO BE
TRUE.
OH, I DON'T KNOW WHY I TRUST YOU, BUT
I DO,
(YES I DO),
OH, I DON'T KNOW WHY I TRUST YOU, BUT
I DO.
GEOFFREY.
DO, DO, DO, DO.
DO, DO, DO, DO.
THERE IS DANGER WITH A STRANGER.

FROM THE MOMENT OF OUR MEETING,
I FELT WE WERE REPEATING
AN ENCOUNTER WE'D ENCOUNTERED ONCE
BEFORE.
ONCE BEFORE.

WHEN OUR GLANCES COINCIDED,
I KNEW FATE HAD BEEN DECIDED.
IT'S A CHEMISTRY YOU KNOW YOU CAN'T
   IGNORE.
   HOPE.
TELL ME MORE!
   GEOFFREY.
LET YOUR HEART START BEATING FASTER.
IT'S THAT WELL-KNOWN LOVE FORECASTER.
LET OUR HEARTS COLLIDE,
THERE'S HAPPINESS IN STORE.
   HOPE and GEOFFREY.
TOGETHER AND CLOSE WE GLIDE,
I'M WARMER THAN TOAST INSIDE,
TOAST INSIDE, TOAST INSIDE!

OH, MY TRUST IN YOU IS UTTER,
WE WILL BE LIKE BREAD AND BUTTER,
LIVING IN A MARMALADE OF TEA FOR TWO.
   HOPE.
(ME FOR YOU).
   GEOFFREY.
OH, I DON'T KNOW WHY I TRUST YOU.
   HOPE.
OH, I DON'T KNOW WHY I TRUST YOU.
   HOPE and GEOFFREY.
OH, I DON'T KNOW WHY I TRUST YOU, BUT
   I DO
(YES I DO)
I DON'T KNOW WHY, BUT I DO!
   (*They dance.*)

OH, I DON'T KNOW WHY I TRUST YOU
OH, I DON'T KNOW WHY I TRUST YOU,
OH, I DON'T KNOW WHY I LOVE YOU, BUT
   I DO
(YES I DO)
I DON'T KNOW WHY, BUT I
(DOODELY, DO, DO, DO/DOODLEY, DO, DO, DO
DOODLEY, DO, BUT I DO!)
   GEOFFREY. My name is Geoffrey.
   HOPE. Of course! Geoffrey. And I'm Hope.
   GEOFFREY. Hello, Hope! (*They kiss.* NIGEL *and* FLINT *enter from library.*)
   NIGEL. Hello, what's this? (HOPE *and* GEOFFREY *break apart.*)
   GEOFFREY. She has a cinder in her eye.
   HOPE. This one!

FLINT. Can I 'elp?

HOPE. It seems to be all right now.

NIGEL. Where are the others?

GEOFFREY. (*Indicating the kitchen, as he and* HOPE *start off in the opposite direction.*) Making tea.

NIGEL. Shall we join them?

HOPE. Well. We were going into the study to . . . to . . .

GEOFFREY. To look for clues.

HOPE. Yes, clues. (*She and* GEOFFREY *exit into the study.*)

NIGEL. They won't find anything important in there.

FLINT. They'll find what they're looking for.

LETTIE. (*Enters.*) Tea's up in the kitchen. (*Exits.*)

FLINT. After you, guvnor.

NIGEL. No, go on ahead, Flint. I'm going up to my room to adjust my cummerbund. (FLINT *exits.* NIGEL *starts up the stairs. When he is certain that* FLINT *is gone, he comes back down to the desk. He finds a paper, which is obviously important. Upstairs,* LADY MP *enters along the landing, frenzied. She looks down and spies* NIGEL. *He does not see her. She steps back into Lord Dudley's doorway. The door opens behind her. She turns and looks into the room, screams and runs down the stairs.* NIGEL, *letter in hand, rushes to the foot of the stairs.*) Lady Grace, is something wrong?

LADY MP. I've just seen Lord Rancour.

NIGEL. Where???

LADY MP. Upstairs!!!

NIGEL. But he's dead!

LADY MP. Yes. I know.

NIGEL. Do you suppose we could have a little talk?

LADY MP. (*Looking away.*) If you don't mind, I'd rather be alone.

NIGEL. (*Approaches* LADY MP.) For this discussion, we should be alone . . . (*He wheels her around to face him.*) Lady Rancour!

LADY MP. Wha . . . what did you call me?

NIGEL. Lady Rancour, I'm on to you and your little game.

LADY MP. What do you mean?

NIGEL. Rumor has it that you, my dear lady, are practically penniless.

LADY MP. That is not true.

NIGEL. It is. You do recognize your own handwriting in this letter to my uncle . . . your ex-husband! (*He reveals the letter he found in the desk.*)

LADY MP. Why should I write Lord Rancour?

NIGEL. To request a loan of several thousand.

LADY MP. . . . Yes! To retain my social position, I must have financial assistance.

NIGEL. (*Reads.*) "Dearest Dudley, you will think it strange, my writing you after all these years. But you are my last hope. Since our divorce . . ."

LADY MP. You needn't go on. We were married!

NIGEL. I never knew my uncle had been married.

LADY MP. It was not a union of love. Dudley was a successful barrister who needed a wife of social prominence. My days and nights were spent in loneliness . . . until I met Shirley, a dashing young lieutenant. Our affair was brief, but beautiful. Dudley found us out and had Shirley sent abroad. I never even knew his last name. I was sent to the south of France until the divorce was final. I stayed on, met Lord Manley-Prowe and tried to forget. And now I am without funds or family.

NIGEL. And old Dudley invited you this weekend to give you your loan.

LADY MP. I had hoped.

NIGEL. And if he refused?

LADY MP. I would have been desperate.

NIGEL. Exactly. Desperate enough to murder.

LADY MP. But, why?

NIGEL. Perhaps you did see him. Perhaps he did refuse.

LADY MP. That is not true.

NIGEL. But if it were? Lady Grace, you have a motive. A motive clearly defined in this letter.

LADY MP. But I did not kill him.

NIGEL. Whether you did or did not does not interest me. My interest lies in the large sum of money my uncle should have left me in his will. A sum we could share . . . if we work together.

LADY MP. Why would you share it with me?

NIGEL. I need your help. I'll tell no one about this letter, if you assist me. We must find my uncle's will. If he has made me his heir, we have no problem. If not, we must destroy the will before anyone sees it. I am, after all, the legal heir.

LADY MP. But how can I help?

NIGEL. I need time to search Dudley's rooms. Don't let anyone come upstairs.

LADY MP. How can I prevent them?

NIGEL. Flirt, swoon, use any womanly device, but . . . I must have time! (*He exits upstairs. Mysterious music underscores his exit.* LADY MP *nervously paces at the bottom of the stairs. The door to the kitchen opens and the* COLONEL *enters. They collide.*)

LADY MP. Oh, you startled me.

COLONEL. I thought you were in your room.

LADY MP. I couldn't sleep.

COLONEL. Well, I can, and, by Jove, I think I will. (*He attempts to pass her, heading upstairs.*)

LADY MP. (*Blocking his way.*) But the night is still young, Colonel.

COLONEL. My dear Lady, the brisk tramp through the elements and the bracer of tea have set me up for a good night's sleep. (*This time he manages to brush past* LADY MP *and heads up the stairs.*)

LADY MP. (*Pulling him back.*) Ah, umh, ah, tell me, Colonel Gillweather, how long have you been in the Army?

COLONEL. Hmmm? All my life, yes, all my life.

LADY MP. It must be a very exciting life.

COLONEL. Nothing like it. Rise at sunup . . . sleep at sunset. Good night, my lady. (*He again starts up the stairs.*)

LADY MP. (*Calls after him.*) Cigarette?

COLONEL. (*Turns to her.*) No, no thank you.

LADY MP. (*Coyly.*) No, I'd like a cigarette.

COLONEL. I beg your pardon. Never touch 'em. Have a havana. (*He steps back down to hand her the cigar.*)

LADY MP. (*Startled.*) Oh. Thank you. (*The* COLONEL *moves up the stairs again.*) Havana. Oh, Havana. Ever been there?

COLONEL. Hmmm? No, not that I recall. But then I've been so many places.

LADY MP. (*During the next few lines, manages to draw him back into the room.*) And with a girl in every port?

COLONEL. No, no, I learned my lesson early in life.

LADY MP. An unhappy love affair?

COLONEL. Yes . . . yes . . . quite.

LADY MP. I completely sympathize, Colonel. I too, had an unhappy love affair. When I was young. As a matter of fact, with a dashing young lieutenant.

COLONEL. (*Not listening to her.*) Ah, I was a lieutenant at the time. She was a beautiful slip of a thing. Every movement filled with Grace. Grace. Grace was her name.

LADY MP. (*Not listening to him.*) My Don Juan was named Shirley.

COLONEL. (*Listening.*) What?

LADY MP. I know, an odd name, Shirley.

COLONEL. His surname?

LADY MP. I never knew.

COLONEL. Your name?

LADY MP. At the time, Grace Rancour.

COLONEL. Grace?

LADY MP. Shirley?

COLONEL. (*Looking her over, aghast.*) Grace?

LADY MP. Shirley? Oh, it's been so long.

COLONEL. Yes, it's been some twenty-odd years, hasn't it?

LADY MP. Yes, twenty years, and now here I am and there you are.

COLONEL. (*Still looking her over.*) Yes, well, there you are. Good night. (*He starts up the stairs again.*)

LADY MP. (*Singing.*)

DA . . . DA . . . DA . . . DUM. DA . . . DA . . .
    DA . . . DUM.

(COLONEL *stops in his tracks.*) Ah, you do remember. (*His back is to her, but he has stopped. Music under.*) The little cafe? . . . the French chanteuse? . . . the vintage wine? . . . Our song.

COLONEL. (*Turns on the steps, singing lustily.*)

DA . . . DA . . . DA . . . DUM. DA . . . DA . . .
    DA . . . DUM.

SONG: THE MAN WITH THE GINGER MOUSTACHE

LADY MP. (*Sings.*)
HE TREATS ME RIGHT.
HE TREATS ME LEFT-OVER,
BUT I ALWAYS HAVE BEEN A PUSH-OVER
FOR A GENTLEMAN WITH PANACHE,
LIKE—THE MAN WITH THE GINGER
    MOUSTACHE.

THE MAN IS CRUEL.
THE MAN IS SWEET.
THE MAN CAN SWEEP ME RIGHT OFF OF MY
    FEET.
ROMANCE CAN GIVE A GIRL A RASH
IF . . . THE MAN HAS A GINGER MOUSTACHE.

I'VE BEEN AROUND WITH MEN OF ALL CLASSES,
KNEW ALL THE TRICKS, AND KNEW ALL THE
    PASSES.
THEN HE APPEARED
AND THE GAME WAS NOT THE SAME.
THIS WAS A DAME THAT HE KNEW HOW TO
    TAME . . . SHAME.

HE TREATS ME RIGHT.
HE TREATS ME WRONG.
BUT IT'S MY SEASON FOR STRINGING ALONG.

ERGO, I'LL HANG ON 'TIL THE CRASH,
LOVING THAT MAN WITH THE GINGER
   MOUSTACHE.
THAT COOL AND PASSIONATE,
FLASHY, IRRATIONAL,
POTENT

MAN WITH THE GINGER MOUSTACHE,
GOT ME GOING AROUND AND AROUND.
CAN'T KEEP BOTH OF MY FEET ON THE
   GROUND.
LOVE THAT LITTLE MOUSTACHE.

    COLONEL. Goodnight. (*He starts upstairs.*)
    LADY MP. There was a child.
    COLONEL. (*He turns and comes down the stairs.*) A child?
    LADY MP. Yes.
    COLONEL. Dudley's?
    LADY MP. Yours . . . and mine.
    COLONEL. Ours?
    LADY MP. Yours and mine.
    COLONEL. A baby?
    LADY MP. A baby.
    COLONEL. A baby child?
    LADY MP. Yes, Shirley.
    COLONEL. Yours. And mine. Baby. Child. Umh, umh, my
dear, sit down. Is there anything I can get you?
    LADY MP. (*Tittering.*) Shirley. That was twenty-one years
ago.
    COLONEL. Brandy!
    LADY MP. Hmmm? Oh, no thank you.
    COLONEL. No. I . . . I'd like a brandy. (*She gets him a
brandy.*) You're sure.
    LADY MP. Yes.
    COLONEL. A father . . . I'm a father.
    LADY MP. Yes, Shirley.
    COLONEL. Grace, I'm a father! Tell me, am I a boy father
or a girl father?
    LADY MP. I never knew. Dudley never allowed me to see the
child.
    COLONEL. Never?
    LADY MP. No. Never. It was part of the bargain. My
shame would never be disclosed and Dudley would raise our
child as his heir. The education and upbringing of the child
was a closely guarded secret. And now Dudley is dead. Oh,
Shirley, we may never know if we are the parents of a boy or
a girl.

COLONEL. Then our child will be Dudley's heir?

LADY MP. Yes. Unless . . .

COLONEL. Unless what?

LADY MP. Unless Nigel finds Dudley's will. He intends destroying it if he isn't the heir. (NIGEL *appears at the head of the stairs.*)

COLONEL. How do you know?

LADY MP. He told me. He wants me to help him . . . and I must.

COLONEL. Must?

NIGEL. (*Loudly, to* LADY MP *and* COLONEL.) Yes, Must! And shall we tell him why, Lady Grace?

LADY MP. Nigel!

NIGEL. (*Holding the letter, descending the stairs.*) Would you like to know the contents of this frantic letter Her Ladyship wrote my uncle?

LADY MP. Nigel! No!

COLONEL. Grace, what does it say?

LADY MP. What about the will? Why don't you tell the Colonel about the will?

NIGEL. Whose business is that but mine? After all, am I not the legal heir? (*They are engaged in a furious argument.* TWEED *enters from the kitchen. She sees them, they see her, then* TWEED *speaks.*)

TWEED. Colonel, you must come back into the kitchen. We've just uncorked the most provocative bottle of Magdelaine '26 I have ever come across. (HOPE *and* GEOFFREY *enter from study.* GEOFFREY *is carrying a gun.*)

HOPE. Miss Tweed, you'll never guess what Geoffrey found! We were examining Clive's body and he found this gun!

TWEED. Examining Clive's body?

GEOFFREY. (*Hands a gun to* TWEED.) Oh, I'm sorry . . . I've probably botched up the fingerprints.

TWEED. Good work, young man. Could this be Lord Rancour's murder weapon? (*The gun is aimed toward the kitchen door.* FLINT *enters, with* LETTIE, *sees* TWEED *aiming the gun at him, reacts.*)

FLINT. Gawd!!

TWEED. There you are, Mr. Flint. Do you recognize this pistol?

FLINT. Never seen it before.

TWEED. Could it have belonged to Clive?

FLINT. I wouldn't know.

TWEED. . . . or perhaps to Lord Rancour?

FLINT. I wouldn't know!

TWEED. Hmmmmm. (*She goes to the desk.*) We'll put it in

the desk, near our other weapon . . . the telephone. (*She has opened desk, finds garden shears.*) What's this? Are these your missing garden shears?

FLINT. Wh . . . how did they get in there?

TWEED. Someone put them there! And . . . possibly . . . someone put this gun on Clive's body. Just as someone put gas into the telephone. But who? (*Music under.*) Now where was I? (*She moves away from others.*)

SONG: SUSPICIOUS

ALL. (*Except* TWEED.)
WHO DID IT? WHO DID IT?
WILL THEY DO IT AGAIN?
WHO'S HEXED? WHO'S NEXT?
THERE'S A CULPRIT TO UNCOVER.
IT IS URGENT TO DISCOVER WHO.
WHO DID IT!

TWEED. (*Spoken.*) Precisely, and what a wealth of clues. (*Singing.*)
THE TELEPHONE'S INGENIOUS BELL. SUSPICIOUS!
THE COLONEL KNOWS HIS GASSES WELL.
    SUSPICIOUS!
THE SERVANTS ARE A CRAFTY PAIR,
THE LADY'S FRENCH: VIN ORDINAIRE . . .
MALICIOUS? SUSPICIOUS! SUSPICIOUS!
THE NEPHEW IS THE UNCLE'S HEIR . . .
    SUSPICIOUS!
THE SWEET YOUNG THING HAS P'ROXIDE HAIR.
    SUSPICIOUS!
THE YOUNG MAN SMUDGED THE FINGERPRINTS.
(THE HOUSE IS FULL OF CLUES AND HINTS.)
SUSPICIOUS! DELICIOUS! SUSPICIOUS!

THRILLING! MISS TWEED IS IN HER ELEMENT.
ADVENTURE IS THE ONLY LIFE FOR ME. (AH
    HA, HEE, HEE!)
CHILLING! A CHILLING ENVIRONMENT.
MALICE, MAYHEM, MYSTERY, MURDER:
JUST MY CUP OF TEA.

HE SAID HE MOVED THE MASTER'S CAR.
    SUSPICIOUS
AND HERE IS SOMETHING FAR TOO FAR
    CAPRICIOUS:
IF SUSPECT FIVE AND SUSPECT THREE HAVE
    KNOWN EACH OTHER PREVIOUSLY,

THEN EVERYTHING IS OBVIOUSLY,
    SUSPICIOUSLY, PERNICIOUSLY
SUSPICIOUS! SUSPICIOUS! SUSPICIOUS!
    SUSPICIOUS!

THRILLING! A THRILLING ENVIRONMENT . . .
ADVENTURE IS THE ONLY LIFE FOR ME . . .
CHILLING! MISS TWEED IS IN HER ELEMENT . . .
MALICE, MAYHEM, MYSTERY, MURDER . . .
MALICE, MAYHEM, MYSTERY, MURDER . . .

(*Thunder booms. Lightning flashes.*)

OTHERS.
A MYSTERY IS HEREABOUT SUSPICIOUS!
WE THINK WE'VE GOT IT FIGURED OUT.
    SUSPICIOUS!
THE ONE WHO KNOWS TOO MUCH INDEED . . .
(*Spoken, accusing, to* TWEED.) Is that old meddling snoop,
Miss Tweed!
    TWEED. What???
    OTHERS.
SUSPICIOUS!
    TWEED. But . . . !!!
    OTHERS.
SUSPICIOUS!
    TWEED. No!!!!
    OTHERS.
SUSPICIOUS! SUSPICIOUS! SUSPICIOUS!
    (*The following lines are spoken individually, by various
    characters.*)
    COLONEL.
THE TELEPHONE'S INGENIOUS BELL!
    HOPE.
THE COLONEL KNOWS HIS GASSES WELL!
    TWEED.
THE NEPHEW IS THE UNCLE'S HEIR!
    NIGEL.
THE SERVANTS ARE A CRAFTY PAIR!
    LETTIE.
THAT MISS HOPE IS RATHER SHADY!
    FLINT.
COULD THE CULPRIT BE THE LADY!
    LADY MP.
THE YOUNG MAN SMUDGED THE FINGERPRINTS!
    GEOFFREY.
BUT THE MISSING SHEARS WERE FLINT'S!

TWEED. Was it Greed?
OTHERS. Was it Tweed?
ALL.
ALL AROUND SUSPICIONS LINGER,
WE ALL POINT THE GUILTY FINGER!
This one did it! That one did it!
This one! That one! This one! That one!
YOU ARE SUSPICIOUS!

(*Thunder booms and the lights go out. A scream is heard and panic reigns.*)

HOPE. Geoffrey! Where are you?
NIGEL. Someone, try the light switch.
GEOFFREY. Strike a match.
NIGEL. The lights!
FLINT. The generator. I'll try the generator.
TWEED. Order! We must have order!
COLONEL. I say, Grace, try the light switch.
LADY MP. Here it is-s-s-s-s-s-s-s-s-s-s-! ! ! ! ! ! ! !

(*As* LADY MP *touches the lightswitch, electricity courses through her body, illuminating her for an instant. As she falls dead, thunder and lightning hit, the lights fade out as the actors move toward her body, and . . .*)

CURTAIN

ACT TWO

Fast Curtain. Minutes later. Lights are still out . . . there is enough illumination just to make out what occurs On-stage. Lightning flashes and thunder, rain is heard.

LADY MP's *body is slowly being dragged through the library door.* TWEED *enters from the kitchen, carrying a lighted candle. She takes a few steps, sees the moving body, and begins calling for help, as she blows out the candle, strikes it beside the fireplace and rushes to the body, grabbing the arms, beginning a tug-of-war. Neither she nor the audience can quite make out who is on the library end of the body.*

TWEED. Let go, you villain, let go!!! Help. Somebody come help me, quickly! (*She gives one hard tug on the body and pulls it and the* COLONEL *through the library door, Onstage. Lights bump up.*) Colonel Gillweather!!!!!

(HOPE, GEOFFREY, NIGEL *and* LETTIE *all enter on the run.*)

HOPE. Miss Tweed!
NIGEL. What's the matter?
LETTIE. What's going on?
COLONEL. Miss Tweed, let's me explain.
TWEED. Please do, Colonel Gillweather. (*To the others.*) He was attempting to remove the remains. (TWEED *still holds* LADY MP's *arms. The* COLONEL *still has her feet.*)
COLONEL. . . . only into the library with the others. (*He is sad.*) Grace. Grace.
TWEED. Oh. I see. Well, then, shall we do it?
GEOFFREY. Miss Tweed, let me . . .
TWEED. No, thank you, Geoffrey. I need the exercise. (TWEED *and* COLONEL *exit into the library with the body.*)
FLINT. (*Runs on from the Servants' Quarters.*) Well, the power's on again.
GEOFFREY. Good work, Flint.
NIGEL. Very good work, Flint.
FLINT. 'Appens all the time.
TWEED. (*Enters.*) Mr. Flint. I see we have electricity.
FLINT. Yes, Miss.
TWEED. How was it repaired?

FLINT. Just fiddled with the generator.
TWEED. Indeed? Is the generator our only source of power?
FLINT. Yes, Miss.
TWEED. I think we'd better have a look. (FLINT *exits into the Servants' Quarters.* COLONEL *enters from library.*) Come along, Colonel.
LETTIE. I'm goin' with you.

(TWEED, COLONEL, LETTIE *follow* FLINT *off.* HOPE *and* GEOFFREY *follow the others to the doorway, arm in arm, but do not exit. They quickly turn about and exit into the study.*)

HOPE. (*As they exit.*) Oh, Geoffrey, you're so naughty!
NIGEL. (*He has been sitting in the desk chair, his back to the audience, wheels around, stands.*) Alone at last! (*He searches every conceivable element of the set while he sings: atop of the mantel, in the desk, around the pouff, etc.*)

SONG: THE LEGAL HEIR

'TWAS IN HIS ROOM MY UNCLE BREATHED
HIS LAST, OFFENSIVE BREATH.
AND HERE'S THE PLACE WHERE LADY GRACE
SHOCKED HERSELF TO DEATH
AND CLIVE WAS ON THE STAIR . . .
THE DOCTOR, OVER THERE . . .
AND I'M THE LEGAL HEIR.

(*Spoken.*) Now, uncle, where's your lovely, lovely will.
    (*Sings.*)
I KNOW WHAT I'M LOOKING FOR,
AND WHAT I'M LOOKING FOR
HAS GOT TO BE YOU.

YOU ARE WHAT I'VE WAITED FOR,
PALPITATED FOR,
MY DREAM WILL COME TRUE.

COME TO ME,
LET ME KNOW YOU'RE MINE.
LET MY LOVE ENSHRINE YOU FOREVER.
I'M THE ONE.
TELL ME I'M THE ONE.
LET NO OTHER ONE BE WITH YOU EVER
I KNOW WHAT I'M LOOKING FOR
AND WHAT I'M LOOKING FOR

HAS GOT TO BE HERE.

(*He dances and earnestly searches for the will. At last, he finds it. The will is rolled up in a decanter on the bar, attached to the stopper.*)

HERE YOU ARE. I HAVE YOU AT LAST.
NOW MY TROUBLED PAST IS CLEARLY PASSE.

HALLELU.
NOW THAT I HAVE YOU,
I'LL GO TO PERU, PERHAPS MANDALAY!

OMIGOD!
OH MY DARK DESPAIR.
UNCLE WASN'T FAIR
I'M NOT THE LEGAL HEIR!
NOT THE LEGAL HEIR!
NOT THE LEGAL HEIR!

(*BONK! NIGEL is hit on the head and driven to the floor by a sconce attached to the post at bottom of staircase. He is dead, will in hand. The sconce zips back into place.*)

COLONEL. (*Enters.*) Umf, Miss Langdon! Miss Langdon? Not here. Probably off somewhere with that disgraceful young chap in his underwear. (*He starts to exit.*) Miss Langdon! Hmmmmmf. What's this? Master Nigel, you look a bit smashed. I say, uh, come, come old man. Up to bed. (*He attempts to help NIGEL up.*) Omigod!— Again? (*He drops NIGEL.*) What's this. (*He picks up the will and crosses down near the pouff.*) It's Lord Rancour's will. "I, Lord Dudley Rancour, being of sound mind and body do hereby, hmmm . . . (*A shrunken head has reared from the top of the pouff. It holds a blowgun in its mouth. The COLONEL hears something, stops, then continues.*) and also . . . (*We hear the swish of a dart, and the head retreats.*) What's this? (*He finds a small dart behind his neck. He inspects the dart, sniffs it, tastes the tip, holds it aloft.*) Inee! Poison commonly used by the Mundurucu tribe of the Upper Amazon. Nasty little devil. (*He looks at his watch.*) Should mean I have about five minutes left.

TWEED. (*Enters from the Servants' Quarters, in a hurry.*) Colonel Gillweather, thank goodness you're here. I have a problem.

COLONEL. You too?

TWEED. Flint pinched me. Directly behind the generator.

COLONEL. What cheek! However, Miss Tweed, I must call your attention to this dart.

TWEED. (*Pulling the* COLONEL *Downstage of the pouff.*) No time for games, Colonel! We have serious matters to contend with. Time is of the essence!

COLONEL. You're telling me! (LETTIE *and* FLINT *enter.*)

LETTIE. Gripper! How could you do such a thing? (HOPE *and* GEOFFREY *have entered, from the study.*)

HOPE. Oh, there you are!

GEOFFREY. We've been . . .

HOPE. He's been . . . ! (*Spying* NIGEL'S *body.*)

TWEED. Nigel! (TWEED *rushes to the body. She is joined by* GEOFFREY *and* FLINT.)

COLONEL. (*Now alone Downstage.*) I've been poisoned, dammit!

LETTIE. Is he dead?

FLINT. Struck down in the prime of life . . .

TWEED. . . . by a heavy metal object, I would say.

HOPE. (*Faintly.*) I don't feel well.

COLONEL. That makes two of us!

LETTIE. (*To* HOPE.) Maybe you should lie down, luv. (LETTIE *leads* HOPE *up the stairs and off. Both are visibly shaken.*)

TWEED. Gentlemen, the library. (GEOFFREY *and* FLINT *carry* NIGEL *into the library. At library door.*) Colonel, could we have a minute alone?

COLONEL. (*Looking at his pocket watch.*) You can have almost two minutes if you like.

TWEED. Well, Colonel, what have you to say for yourself?

COLONEL. I found this in my neck.

TWEED. (*Inspecting the dart.*) Inee! That means you have five minutes to go.

COLONEL. Not any more.

TWEED. Were you able to see who did it?

COLONEL. I don't know, but the answer may be here. (*He hands her the will.*)

TWEED. Dudley's will. (*She begins reading it.*)

COLONEL. Yes. Dudley's legal heir is . . .

TWEED. Hope Langdon, but how?

COLONEL. Dudley's adopted daughter. My love-child. Her mother was Grace Rancour Manley-Prowe.

TWEED. (*Looking over her shoulder, toward the library.*) Grace *Rancour* Manley-Prowe? Does Miss Langdon know about this?

COLONEL. (*Looks at watch.*) No time for that question. (*While he counts down, he lies on the floor, positioning himself before the library door.*) In fact, no time at all. Ten . . .

nine . . . eight . . . seven . . . six . . . five . . . four . . .
three . . . two . . . one . . . (*He looks at his watch, taps it,
shakes it at his ear, says.*) It must be fast. (*He dies.*)

TWEED. Tsk . . . tsk . . . tsk . . . tsk. (*She hears the
voices of* FLINT *and* GEOFFREY *coming from the library. She
quickly hides the will in her pocket.*)

GEOFFREY. (*Enters, with* FLINT.) Miss Tweed, I . . .
(*Gasps.*) . . . the Colonel!

TWEED. (*Nods.*) Yes.

GEOFFREY. But how?

TWEED. A poisoned dart.

GEOFFREY. No!

TWEED. (*Nods. Archly.*) With dignity, men. (FLINT *and*
GEOFFREY *pull him by the arms to the library.* LETTIE *enters
halfway down the stairs, watching them, awestruck.*) C'est la
guerre!

LETTIE. (*Rushing down the stairs.*) I'm gettin' out of ere!

TWEED. Now, Lettie, don't be rash!

LETTIE. Rash? I'm not goin' to be the next one dragged into
that library. They're droppin' like flies. I'm gettin' out if I
'ave to swim the lake.

TWEED. You're just excited, my dear.

LETTIE. Excited? Of course I'm excited. With five of us left,
the odds are not very good for me, are they?

TWEED. You're right, my dear, when you consider that one
of us is the murderer.

LETTIE. Like I said, I'm leavin'.

TWEED. Now, Lettie . . .

LETTIE. (*Backing away.*) Hands off, suspect! (FLINT *and*
GEOFFREY *enter.*)

TWEED. What?

LETTIE. Yes! I suspect you as much as 'im or 'im or 'er.
(*Indicates* FLINT, GEOFFREY *and upstairs,* HOPE.) Who knew
this 'ouse inside and out?

FLINT. Now wait a minute, who knew the Master inside and
out? (*Accusations are flying.*)

TWEED. Please!

FLINT. Just what do you . . . ?

GEOFFREY. Lettie, please calm down.

LETTIE. (*To* GEOFFREY.) And who are you? Appearin' out
of nowhere! (*To* FLINT.) I wouldn't trust 'im for a minute!
(*To* GEOFFREY.) You foxy Oxford coxs'n!!

GEOFFREY. Foxy Oxford coxs'n?? That's easy for *you* to
say! (*They are now all heatedly talking,* TWEED *trying to
calm them.*)

TWEED. Please! Please! Please! (*She gives a pinch on their behinds and they all stop.*) We are all under suspicion. None of us should forget that.

LETTIE. I haven't forgotten that, and I'm going to pack this minute! (*She exits into the Servants' Quarters.*)

TWEED. Lettie is right. We should pack. And be prepared to leave as soon as is climactically possible. (*Thunder booms.*)

FLINT. It'll be a while.

TWEED. Nevertheless, pack. (*She exits upstairs.*)

FLINT. (*With a shrug.*) Pack. (*He exits into the kitchen.*)

GEOFFREY. Pack? Pack? Where is my knappack . . . knapsack? Ohhh. (*He exits into the study. Thunder and lightning. HOPE is heard Offstage: "Geoffrey!" Thunder and lightning again. HOPE enters. "Geoffrey!" Thunder and lightning.*)

HOPE. (*Appears at the top of the stairs.*) Geoffrey! Yoohoo! Yoo-hoo!

SONG: YOU FELL OUT OF THE SKY

(YOO—) WHO WOULD HAVE BELIEVED IT
    COULD HAPPEN,
THAT A DREAM COULD COME TRUE WITH SUCH
    EASE:
LIKE ORPHEUS OUT OF THE UNDERWORLD
OR NEPTUNE OUT OF THE SEAS.

YOU FELL OUT OF THE SKY,
AND SUDDENLY CUPID AIMED HIS ARROW AND
    SHOT ME, GOT ME.
MY BLUES BID ME GOODBYE,
THE MOMENT THAT YOU FELL OUT OF THE SKY.
    (*The chandelier starts to fall then stops as HOPE moves from underneath it. She does not see the chandelier.*)

YOU FELL OUT OF THE SKY
WHILE SEARCHING FOR CLUES TO USE, YOU
    STARTED TO TEASE ME, PLEASE ME:
I KNEW INSTANTLY WHY,
THE REASON WAS YOU FELL OUT OF THE SKY.
    (*The chandelier moves again. HOPE moves away. Chandelier stops.*)

MY HEART IS POUNDING MADLY:
IT BEATS A WILD TATTOO,
EXPLOSIONS ROAR INSIDE ME:

INSISTING, "I LOVE YOU."
TRUE, HOW CAN I DENY, THE UNION OF YOU
   WITH ME
COULD NEVER BE TRAGIC, IT'S MAGIC!
I DO IS MY REPLY
THANK HEAVEN THAT YOU FELL OUT OF THE
   SKY.
(*The chandelier falls to the floor, but* HOPE *has moved away.
She gasps and screams.* GEOFFREY *enters on the run.*) Oh,
Geoffrey!

GEOFFREY. Are you quite all right?

HOPE. (*Becomes hysterical.*) All right? How could I possibly
be all right? This house . . . these people . . . it's a mad-
house. I can't stand it any longer, I can't stand it. I can't! I
can't! I can't!

GEOFFREY. (*Holds her, comforting her.*) Darling, darling,
darling!

LETTIE. (*Enters with her valise.*) At it again?

TWEED. (*Enters.*) The chandelier!

GEOFFREY. It barely missed her! (FLINT *enters.*)

LETTIE. What happened?

FLINT. (*Inspecting the chandelier.*) The chandelier fell. The
rope's not cut . . . it must have slipped.

TWEED. I doubt that this was an accident.

LETTIE. (*To* HOPE.) That means you were supposed to be
next!

HOPE. Oh, Geoffrey!

GEOFFREY. Don't worry. I'm here.

HOPE. But where were you five minutes ago?

TWEED. Where were we *all*, five minutes ago? (*Everyone
stops and thinks, backing away from each other. All feel alone,
without trust. Strains of mystery music play.*)

FLINT. (*Becoming too nervous.*) I'd better get this thing out
of 'ere. (*He goes to the chandelier rope, which is slightly Offstage, Up Right. He can be seen, pulling on the rope. The
chandelier slowly rises.*)

TWEED. Lettie, I think we'll all be wanting tea.

HOPE. Yes, please.

LETTIE. Yeah, I guess you need it. (HOPE *smiles wanly.*)
Who's going to come with me?

GEOFFREY. (*To* HOPE.) I'll be right back. (*He exits into the
kitchen with* LETTIE.)

TWEED. My dear, tea will be a few minutes. We could take
advantage of this time to put your things together. (*She leads*
HOPE *up the stairs.*)

HOPE. But what about Geoffrey?

TWEED. He'll be along in a minute. (GEOFFREY *and* LETTIE *enter from kitchen.*)

GEOFFREY. Well, we've got the gas on.

LETTIE. But we need a match to light it. (GEOFFREY *goes Upstage to* FLINT, *to get a match from him.*) Oh, where are you off to?

TWEED. I have a few more things to bring down. (*She continues leading* HOPE *up the stairs.*)

HOPE. And I'm going to get ready to leave.

LETTIE. I'm packed already. And as soon as I get your tea made, I'm gettin' out of 'ere.

GEOFFREY. Here's your match, Lettie.

HOPE. Geoffrey. I, uh, I always have trouble closing my valise.

GEOFFREY. Oh, I'm a crackerjack at valises. (*He rushes up the stairs to join* HOPE *and* TWEED. *They exit.*)

LETTIE. But what about the tea?

FLINT. (*Spies* LETTIE *alone on Stage, crosses down to her.*) I'll give you any assistance you need .

LETTIE. I don't need any assistance you could give me. Gripper! (*She starts to exit into the kitchen.*)

FLINT. Maybe you do. There's a boat. (LETTIE *stops.*)

LETTIE. Eh!

FLINT. (*Slowly.*) There's . . . a . . . boat!

LETTIE. Eohhh!

SONG: DINGHY

FLINT.
I'D ALMOST FORGOT ITS EXISTENCE,
BUT IT'S SITTING THERE, READY TO USE.
IT'S STILL CAPABLE OF DISTANCE
SO STEP RIGHT UP, AND PUT ON YOUR CRUISING
    SHOES.
I'VE GOT A TEENY LITTLE DINGHY
FOR YOU TO SEE,
BUT MY TEENY LITTLE DINGHY'S
BIG ENOUGH FOR ONLY YOU AND ME.

LETTIE. (*Spoken.*) Does it have a motor?

FLINT. (*Spoken.*) In a manner of speakin' . . . (*Sings.*)
IT'S A TEENY LITTLE DINGHY.
AND IT'S SHIPSHAPE . . .
JUST A TEENY LITTLE DINGHY
SITTIN' THERE TO USE IN OUR ESCAPE.

LETTIE.
ESCAPE? ESCAPE? DID YOU SAY ESCAAA-
    AAAAPE???

COME, LET US GO,
LET US FLY, LET US DISAPPEAR.
NOW IS THE TIME FOR THE TWO OF US
TO GET OUR BLOOMIN', BLINKIN' YOU-KNOW-
     WHATS-IS
OUT OF HERE.
DID YOU SAY ESCAPE?
YES HE SAID ESCAAAAAAAAPE!!!
OH, YOU'RE WONDERFUL!
     FLINT. (*Spoken.*) I ain't used it since last winter, but I
think I can get it goin' again.
     LETTIE. Not a word to anyone else!
     FLINT. Oh, look at you . . . conspirin' with a gripper!
     LETTIE. I was only jokin' . . . Flint! Think! (*Sings.*)
US IN YOUR TEENY LITTLE DINGHY,
NO CHAPERONE.
PLUS IN YOUR TEENY LITTLE DINGHY,
LUCKY YOU AND I WILL BE ALONE.
     FLINT. Alone? ALONE? DID YOU SAY ALOOOO-
OOONE???
     LETTIE. Yes, but . . .
     FLINT. (*Sings.*)
COME, LET US GO,
LET US FLY, LET US DISAPPEAR.
NOW IS THE TIME FOR THE TWO OF US
TO GET OUR BLOOMIN', BLINKIN' YOU-KNOW-
     WHATS-IS
OUT OF HERE.
DID YOU SAY ALONE?
YES, SHE SAID ALOOOOOOOONE!!!

LETTIE.	FLINT.
ESCAAAAAAPE???	ALOOOOOOOONE??
ESCAAAAAAPE???	ALOOOOOOOONE??

     FLINT and LETTIE.
IF YOU'RE GOT A TEENY LITTLE DINGHY
YOU MUST RECALL
THAT A TEENY LITTLE DINGHY'S
BETTER THAN NO DINGHY AT ALL!
     LETTIE. (*Anxious to leave.*) Let's get going!
     FLINT. Hold on, girl. I have to look for the oars. You get
your things together . . . I'll be back in five minutes. (*He
exits.*)
     LETTIE. (*She puts on her coat.*) I'm gettin' out of 'ere!
(*Thunder booms.*) I'd have swum the lake if I'd had to . . .
Lunatics and lechers, that's what they all are. I'll be a lot safer

out there with 'im. Why doesn't he hurry? I want to get out
of here. (*She discovers a letter in her coat pocket.*) What's
this? (*She reads.*) "Dear Lord Rancour, as your solicitor, I
must insist that you stop hiding very large sums of money in
the antique four-foot tall Ming vase with the giant teal blue
dragon and persimmon flowers . . ." (*She shrugs, crumples
the note and drops it on the floor. Then, realizing she is standing in front of the vase, she is frozen in shock, but recovers
and turns to dive into the vase. WHOOOOOSH!!! She dis-
appears into the vase. Vase belches out one shoe.* Tweed *appears at the head of the stairs, carrying her wicker.*) Lettie!
. . . (*She calls.*) Lettie, if you've finished with the tea, I
could use some help with my wickers. Where can that girl be?
(*She struggles halfway down with the wicker, sets it down
and attempts to pull it down, derriere in the air.*)

Flint. (*Enters, sees the derriere, trips up the stairs, putting
his arms around* Tweed.) May I be of assistance?

Tweed. (*Whirling around.*) Mr. Flint! (*She passes him,
going down the stairs.*) You may handle my wicker, nothing
more.

Flint. (*Scurries down with the wicker.*) I'll handle anything
you like, Miss.

Tweed. I'm afraid not, Mr. Flint. You see, I haven't forgotten the incident behind the generator.

Flint. Oh. And neither have I.

Tweed. Well, try, Mr. Flint, try.

Flint. Oh, I'm always in there tryin'.

Tweed. Mr. Flint. Mr. Flint. Remember, you are a gentleman, and I am a lady.

Flint. (*Chasing her around the desk chair.*) I wouldn't have
it any other way.

Tweed. Mr. Flint!

Geoffrey. (*Appears at the head of the stairs.*) I say, what
about tea?

Tweed. (*Composing herself, getting away from* Flint.)
Tea? Tea? Lettie! Lettie! Where is that girl? You don't suppose she . . . no, no, her valise is here. And, what have we
here? (*She picks up shoe. She picks up the crumpled letter.*
Geoffrey *comes down the stairs.*) What *have* we here? (*She
reads.*) Gentlemen, something's afoot. (Flint *and* Geoffrey
read over her shoulder.) Another diabolical plot!

Flint. You don't think she would have?

Geoffrey. She couldn't have . . .

Tweed. (*Goes to vase, peers in.*) She did! (Flint *and*
Geoffrey *are shocked.*) Gentlemen.

FLINT and GEOFFREY. The library! (TWEED *drops shoe in the vase. Solemnly,* FLINT *and* GEOFFREY *take up the vase and exit with it toward the library.*)

TWEED. Damn clever, those Chinese.

HOPE. (*Appears at the head of the stairs.*) Oh, Miss Tweed, have you seen Geoffrey? I sent him for my tea.

TWEED. Tea?

HOPE. Yes, you know. The tea that Lettie was making.

TWEED. Lettie was unable to complete that task.

HOPE. Why?

TWEED. Another fiendishly concocted device.

HOPE. Oh, Miss Tweed. (*Gasps, runs down the stairs to* TWEED. *She stops, looking around, half-fearing* TWEED.) Oh, I wish Geoffrey were here.

TWEED. He'll be here in a moment. Why don't you sit down? I do wish we had that tea.

FLINT. (*Entering, overhears* TWEED.) I'll make the tea. I could do with some myself. (*He stops at the kitchen door, taking out his pipe.* GEOFFREY *enters.*)

HOPE. (*Running to* GEOFFREY.) Geoffrey!

GEOFFREY. Are you all right?

HOPE. I will be. After I've had my tea. (FLINT *takes out a match and strikes it.*) Flint is making it. (FLINT *exits into the kitchen, holding the lighted match.*)

GEOFFREY. I wonder if Lettie turned off the gas. (*All three freeze. Beat. VAROOOM! An explosion is heard. Under the kitchen door, a small amount of smoke pours out. Hold for Offstage clatter of dishes and pots.*)

TWEED. (*Goes to the kitchen door, relegating* FLINT *to the kitchen forever.*) Goodnight, sweet Flint.

GEOFFREY. (*After a moment.*) I feel terribly guilty. I should have remembered the gas.

TWEED. Don't blame yourself. Accidents do happen.

HOPE. That's right! It was an accident, wasn't it?

GEOFFREY. And I feel I'm to blame.

TWEED. No, Geoffrey. (*To* HOPE.) I understand what you're saying, my dear. Mr. Flint wasn't murdered!

HOPE. That's right.

TWEED. Eight deaths have occurred in this house tonight. Seven obviously premeditated. The eighth, Flint, was accidental. A provident twist of fate.

GEOFFREY. Come again?

TWEED. Provident for us that fate struck him down before his plans for our deaths came to fruition.

GEOFFREY. Then, Flint is the murderer?

TWEED. Precisely.

HOPE. (*To* GEOFFREY, *as if he should have known it all along.*) Yes, dear.

TWEED. Oh, I've suspected him for some time.

GEOFFREY. Yes. Living here, he would know the house, well, better than anyone.

HOPE. But . . . have you considered his motive?

TWEED. Yes. Insanity.

GEOFFREY. Really?

TWEED. It's the only possible solution. Pathological killers need no motivation.

GEOFFREY. I've heard that, too.

HOPE. Listen! (*They listen.*) The rain. It's stopped.

GEOFFREY. We'll soon be able to leave.

TWEED. It's almost dawn. We'll wait until sunup.

HOPE. I should finish packing.

TWEED. (*Takes the will from her pocket, hands it to* HOPE.) Before you do anything else, I think you should read this. (*To* GEOFFREY.) I've been waiting for the proper time to give it to her.

HOPE. (*Looking over the will.*) Lord Rancour's will? Why should I read it?

TWEED. Turn to the second page.

HOPE. (*Reading the second page.*) I think I should sit down. (*She sits.*)

GEOFFREY. (*Goes to her.*) Hope, is anything wrong?

TWEED. On the contrary. Miss Langdon is heir to the Rancour fortune.

GEOFFREY. What?

HOPE. That's what it says, Geoffrey. Read it. (*She hands* GEOFFREY *the will.*) But why, Miss Tweed? I don't understand.

TWEED. You are the love child of Colonel Gillweather and Lady Manley-Prowe. Your birth was, unfortunately, illegitimate.

HOPE. Does that mean I'm a . . . Ba—

TWEED. (*She clasps her hand over* HOPE's *mouth, so that she need not say the offensive word.*) Yes, my dear. But a very rich one. You are Lord Rancour's adopted daughter. For reasons of his own, he preferred to remain anonymous.

GEOFFREY. You never knew?

HOPE. I hadn't an inkling.

TWEED. Dudley wanted it that way.

HOPE. Then that's why I was invited here this weekend. I'd wondered.

TWEED. Yes, my dear. Hope, you're a very lucky girl.

HOPE. Yes, I am. And I am lucky to have such a good friend in you, Miss Tweed.

GEOFFREY. And you are a masterly detective.
TWEED. Tut! Tut!
HOPE. Tell us! However do you do it?
TWEED. Books!!

SONG: I OWE IT ALL

BOOKS ABOUT SUSPENSE, MYSTERY AND
    MURDER!
HOPE. Whatever do you mean, Miss Tweed?
    TWEED.
I OWE IT ALL TO AGATHA CHRISTIE,
AND ARTHUR CONAN DOYLE.
CHARLIE CHAN AND MARY ROBERTS RINEHART
TAUGHT ME CRIMINOLOGY IS DEFINITELY A
    FINE ART.
AND A NOD OF THE HEAD TO WILLIAM
    SHAKESPEARE
THAT WITCHES' BREW CONTAINED A CLUE OR
    TWO.
I OWE IT ALL TO AGATHA CHRISTIE.
AGGIE, MERCI BEAUCOUP.
    GEOFFREY. Oh, Miss Tweed! . . . (TWEED *covers his mouth
and goes on with song.*)
    TWEED.
I OWE A BIT TO WILKIE COLLINS
AND GARDNER, STANLEY, ERLE
I HAVE LEARNT DETECTION FROM THE
    MASTERS.
WHEN A CULPRIT'S ON THE LOOSE,
I'M NOT A NOVICE AT DEDUCING
WHAT, WHERE, AND WHY AND WHO HAS DONE
    IT,
BUT I MUST GIVE MY MENTOR HER DUE:
AGATHA CHRISTIE, I GET A BIT MISTY,
THINKING WHAT I OWE YOU.
    HOPE and GEOFFREY. (*Repeat the first Verse.*)
I OWE IT ALL, etc.
    TWEED.
(THERE'S) THE HOUNDS OF THE BASKERVILLES,
AND DR. WATSON, TOO,
AND EVERY DETECTIVE BOOK THAT E'ER
CONTAINED A CLUE.
ROGER ACKROYD, THIRTEENTH GUEST,
AND BALDPATE WITH ITS KEYS.
THE AFTER-HOUSE, THE BAT, AND ALL
THOSE OTHER MYSTERIES.

Tweed, Hope, and Geoffrey.
(AND WITH) A NOD OF THE HEAD TO WILLIAM
    SHAKESPEARE . . .
THERE'S MUCH ADO IN RICHARD 3 AND 2.
Tweed.
I OWE IT ALL TO AGATHA CHRISTIE . . .
    Hope and Geoffrey.
AND WE OWE IT ALL TO YOU.
    Tweed.
MY HEART IS POUNDING MADLY.
IT BEATS A WILD TATTOO.
EXPLOSIONS ROAR INSIDE ME
ALL SAYING I LOVE . . .
    Tweed, Hope, and Geoffrey. (Hope *and* Geoffrey *have
gotten three hats from the closet.*)
AGATHA, AGGIE, AGATHA, AGGIE
YOU TAUGHT THE THREE OF US TO CARRY ON.

DON'T BE AFRAID, WHEN YOU CAN BE
    COURAGEOUS,
WHY BE AFRAID,
HIGH SPIRITS ARE CONTAGIOUS,
CARRY, CARRY, WE SHALL CARRY . . .
    (*Softly.*)
WE OWE IT ALL TO AGATHA CHRISTIE,
AND ARTHUR CONAN DOYLE.
    Tweed. (*Speaks.*) You bet your bumbershoot!
    Tweed, Hope, and Geoffrey.
CHARLIE CHAN AND MARY ROBERTS RINEHART
TAUGHT US CRIMINOLOGY IS DEFINITELY A
    FINE ART. WITH A NOD OF THE HEAD TO
    WILLY SHAKESPEARE.
THAT WITCHES' BREW CONTAINED A CLUE OR
    TWO.
OH, WE OWE IT ALL TO AGATHA CHRISTIE,
AGATHA CHRISTIE,
WE'RE ALL OF US MISTY.
AGATHA CHRISTIE . . .
AGATHA CHRISTIE, GOD BLESS YOU!!!

(*All exit to the library at the end of song.* Tweed, *followed by*
    Hope *and* Geoffrey, *enter from library.*)

Hope. Oh, I feel so much better.
    Tweed. I do, too. In fact, I feel very creative. Since we have
some time, I think I'll paint . . . paint, Geoffrey! Yes, you'd

make the perfect model. (*Getting her easel and canvas from study.*)

GEOFFREY. Do you really think I would?

TWEED. Yes, yes. A perfect specimen. (TWEED *gets her pallet and brush.*)

HOPE. Oh, Miss Tweed, do let me watch!

TWEED. (*Setting up her easel and bringing desk chair to it.*) No, this is going to be my little surprise for the two of you.

HOPE. Oh. Then I won't bother you. I'll just pop upstairs and finish my packing. (*She pops upstairs and exits.*)

GEOFFREY. Shouldn't I go with her?

TWEED. There's no danger now.

GEOFFREY. You're right. Well, what do I do?

TWEED. Stand in a comfortable position and hold it. (GEOFFREY *positions himself on a line with* TWEED, *who has seated herself at the easel. He assumes an awkward pose.*) I know, make a muscle! (*He makes a muscle.*) That's it. Now, don't move. (*She begins painting with fervor.*) You're doing splendidly. Let's see, for the hair, a little amber, a tat of umbre. Mixing is so important, you know . . . (*She is busy at her mixing and painting.*) You and Hope seem . . . very close. You're sure you've never met before?

GEOFFREY. No. Never. It's a happy coincidence, our meeting like this.

TWEED. It's been an evening of coincidence. For instance, Hope's *real* parents being here. And your unexpected arrival . . . coincidence. Like . . . your suggestion that we try the telephone. Hmmm. You found the gun on Clive's body, and *you* accidentally . . . left the gas on.

GEOFFREY. (*Still in his pose.*) I do feel awful about that . . . but we got our murderer!

TWEED. No, we didn't, Geoffrey. It wasn't Flint.

GEOFFREY. (*Breaking his pose.*) But . . . there are only three of us left. You're not suspecting me??!?

TWEED. Muscles up! (GEOFFREY *poses again.*) No, not you, dear. I was talking about coincidence: you were the uninvited guest. Whereas, I have been *planning* this weekend for weeks and weeks.

GEOFFREY. (*Suddenly suspicious of* TWEED.) You've been . . . ?? (*He makes a slight move.*) I . . . I'd better see what's keeping Hope.

TWEED. Don't move! (GEOFFREY *snaps back into his pose.*) Hope is quite safe . . . she has nothing to worry about. (*Sudden thought.*) Of course, the house! I've deduced it, Geoffrey . . . I know who the murderer is!! (*From the wall behind* TWEED, *the remaining spear descends rapidly, grasps the end of the muffler in its teeth.*)

GEOFFREY. Really? Who?

TWEED. I should have known it all along. It's elementary. All it required was putting this and that together. Now I've got the answer. Geoffrey the murderer is . . . (*The spear pulls rapidly up on the muffler, strangling* TWEED. *Her head falls on her shoulder. She is dead. The muffler is still caught in the teeth of the spear.*)

GEOFFREY. (*Still in his pose.*) Who, Miss Tweed? Who? (*He turns and sees* TWEED.) Omigod!

(GEOFFREY *rushes to* TWEED, *jerks the muffler free from the spear, which quickly retreats. He bends over* TWEED, *loosening the muffler. In her chair,* GEOFFREY *wheels* TWEED *toward the library door, as* HOPE *enters above.* HOPE *freezes, watching, then speaks quite seriously when he returns from the library.*)

HOPE. It was you all the time!

GEOFFREY. (*Looking up.*) What??

HOPE. You're the one. You're the murderer!

GEOFFREY. Hope, what's the matter with you?

HOPE. What a fool I've been!

GEOFFREY. Darling, let me explain.

HOPE. Explain? I've just seen you with my own two eyes. I was blind not to have seen it before.

GEOFFREY. You're making a mistake.

HOPE. I suppose I'm next?

GEOFFREY. (*Advances to her on the stairs.*) Hope, stop it!

HOPE. (*Pulling away past him, clearing the easel.*) Get away from me!

GEOFFREY. (*Following her.*) Hope!

HOPE. The chandelier! Of course! You've already tried once, haven't you?

GEOFFREY. (*Advancing.*) No!

HOPE. (*Still retreating.*) This time, it won't be so easy.

GEOFFREY. (*Still advancing.*) Hope, you're hysterical!

HOPE. (*Backing against the fireplace, picks up a poker.*) Take one more step! (*She raises the poker threateningly.*)

GEOFFREY. (*Aghast.*) You're mad!

HOPE. (*Advancing on* GEOFFREY.) I mean it, Geoffrey.

GEOFFREY. You're acting like a lunatic! (*He retreats.*)

HOPE. It's very easy to kill, Geoffrey.

GEOFFREY. (*Gasps.*) Then you must be the murderer!

HOPE. (*Laughs hysterically.*) Don't try to confuse me. (HOPE *retreats.*)

GEOFFREY. (*Following her towards fireplace.*) Hope, how could you?

HOPE. I don't want to hear any more.

GEOFFREY. But, Hope, I love you.

HOPE. (*Raises the poker above her head.*) Geoffrey, stop it! (GEOFFREY *grabs at the mantel. The* [*over the mantel*] *portrait swings out to reveal a Gramophone on a base. She drops the poker.*) Geoffrey, behind you! Look! A Gramophone! (GEOFFREY *goes to it.*)

GEOFFREY. It has a record on it.

HOPE. Do you think we should play it?

GEOFFREY. Of course.

(GEOFFREY *places the needle on the record. He and* HOPE *back away slightly. From the Victrola is heard: static; scratchy sounds; and then the voice of a crotchety old man.*)

HOPE. Geoffrey, it needs cranking up.

GEOFFREY. Of course. (*Cranking the Victrola.*)

RECORD. (*Speeding up.*) . . . the invitation to the others . . . My dearest Hope . . .

HOPE. Whose voice is that?

RECORD. . . . this is your foster father, Dudley Rancour, speaking . . . (HOPE *gasps.*) welcome to Rancour's Retreat. Yes, my dear, I am the culprit.

HOPE. But, why?

RECORD. I shall explain. You are now of legal age and can inherit my estate without the hindrance of parents or guardian interfering in your future happiness. Better you remain an orphan. The Colonel and Manley-Prowe have been disposed of, and, I, being an old hand at the Bar . . . have tried and convicted myself . . .

HOPE. He took his own life!

RECORD. . . . and have taken my own life, as well.

GEOFFREY. (*To* HOPE.) What about the others?

RECORD. There were three others who knew of your illegitimacy: Clive; Dr. Grayburn, who delivered you; and Miss Tweed. (*During this speech,* GEOFFREY *pours wine into two snifters. Wine is on the table Down Right of the library door.*) Tweed, that old ninny, was your nanny . . .

HOPE. No.

RECORD. . . . for the first six months of your life. Being a snoop, when she learned of your true identity, no doubt she would have come to all the proper, or improper, conclusions. Nigel would have contested the will; Lettie was blackmailing me, for personal reasons; and Flint . . . was a gripper. That is the why. Would you like to know how I did it?

HOPE and GEOFFREY. Yes!!!

RECORD. Then turn me over! (GEOFFREY *turns the* RECORD *over.*) Here is how I did it . . . in every instance, I had an accomplice: the victim, himself! . . . For example: Clive had a penchant for punctuality. Dinner was always announced, from the stair, at precisely 7:15. The explosion was triggered for . . .

HOPE. (*To* GEOFFREY.) 7:15!

RECORD. . . . precisely! . . . Nigel and Lettie had one thing in common. Greed. Greed led Nigel to the will and Lettie to the vase. (*Gleefully.*) I must tell you about the vase.

HOPE. Geoffrey, I've heard enough. Turn down the sound. (GEOFFREY *turns down the volume.*) He did it all for me.

GEOFFREY. He had planned everything. Except, of course, my being here.

HOPE. (*Embraces* GEOFFREY.) Oh, Geoffrey!

GEOFFREY. To us! (*They down the wine. Birds are heard chirping.*)

HOPE. Listen. It must be morning. (*She runs upstairs, throws open the drapes.* GEOFFREY *opens the front door. Sunlight pours in.*) Geoffrey, look, it's a new day.

SONG: NEW DAY

HERE IS THE NEW DAY WE'VE WAITED FOR
IT'S A NEW DAY, YOURS AND MINE.
GEOFFREY. (*Speaks.*) Oh, Hope! (*Sings.*)
WE'LL START A NEW LIFE ON THIS NEW DAY'
AND A NEW SUN WILL SHINE.
GEOFFREY and HOPE.
HAND IN HAND, WE WILL GREET THE WORLD
AS WE SING ALONG OUR WAY.
RAISE UP YOUR VOICES AND JOIN OUR SONG,
IT'S A NEW, NEW DAY!
CHOIR, GEOFFREY and HOPE.
HERE IS THE NEW DAY WE'VE WAITED FOR
IT'S A NEW DAY, YOURS AND MINE.
WE'LL START A NEW LIFE ON THIS NEW DAY,
AND A NEW SUN WILL SHINE.
(*Both start to feel the effects of the poison.*)
CHOIR. (*Alone.*)
HAND IN HAND, WE WILL GREET THE WORLD
AS WE SING ALONG OUR WAY.
RAISE UP YOUR VOICES AND JOIN OUR SONG,
VOICE ON RECORD. . . . and knowing that old Flint habitually takes nips of the wine from the crystal decanter, I have liberally laced it with arsenic. And so my dear Hope, my deeds

are done. The world is yours. It's a new day . . . new day
new day . . . (*The record sticks. Both fall to the floor and
die.*)
    CHOIR.
IT'S A NEW, NEW DAY!

CURTAIN

"I OWE IT ALL"—Finale and calls.

NOTES ON SPECIAL EFFECTS
Clive's Death:
    A flash powder "bomb" is contained in a 20 gal. can and
located under the stair landing. A heating register mounted in
the floor of the landing permits smoke to escape. Clive stands
on this register when he announces "Dinner is served." The
explosion is triggered by the electrician. Containing the bomb
in the can focuses the smoke up through the register in a
column. The sound of the explosion should be loud enough to
startle the audience.
Breakaway Railing for Clive's Death:
    The effect desired is this: the "bomb" under the landing goes
off, kills Clive, who falls forward "through" the railing. We
accomplish this by hinging a section of the railing like a gate.
The unhinged end was held in place by a friction latch so that
the weight of Clive's body opened the "gate" and he could
fall forward to the Stage floor. Later, Miss Tweed, while inspecting the scene of Clive's death during the song "Something's Afoot," restores the "gate" to its closed position and
secures it with barrel bolts. The barrel bolts hold the railing
together solidly for the rest of the show. The bolts are, of
course, open at the top of the show so that the railing is set for
the fall, held only by the friction latch.
Lethal Telephone:
    Telephone bell sound required Stage Left. Dr. Grayburn
searches for source of the ringing. A prop man behind the
wall opens a panel in the wall and pushes out a sliding palette
on which is mounted the telephone. One end of a hose is attached near the mouthpiece of the phone and runs Offstage
through a hole in the flat and is attached to a smoke generat-
ing machine with a bellows attachment, which, on cue, blows
smoke through the hose and "gasses" the good doctor.
Electrocution:
    We cut a square hole in the platform near the main en-
trance to the house and fitted a piece of ¾" Plexiglas in the
hole to support walking. A strobelight under the platform

shoots up through the plexi illuminating Lady MP from below. If necessary, the square of plexi can be concealed under a throw rug. Lady MP kicks the rug aside during the blackout before the electrocution.

Nigel's Death:

A lighted torchiere, mounted on the newel post at the foot of the stairs, is operated by a prop man Offstage. A rigging of steel cable and pulleys allow the torch to fall sideways and hit Nigel as he finishes his song at the foot of the stairs.

The Pouff:

The pouff rolls a few feet, following the Colonel, and stops. The head rises from the Center of the pouff, facing front. The head then turns to face the Colonel and the orchestra supplies a sound effect for the dart. The head then turns front again and descends into the pouff, which then rolls back to position. This is operated by a prop man from beneath the stage through a small hole cut in the deck. The hole is concealed by the pouff itself at both extremes of its travel. It is not necessary for the pouff to roll.

Chandeliers:

There are two chandeliers. The chandelier Stage Right does not move. The one Stage Left has four trims. It plays throughout at high trim except for the song "You Fell Out of the Sky." After the first verse of the song, the chandelier falls a couple of feet as Hope moves from under it. After the second verse, it falls another two feet. At the end of the song it falls to within a few inches of the floor, barely missing Hope. Flint later fakes hoisting it and it returns to high trim. Neither chandelier is wired electrically. For all three falls, a ratchet sound will give added reality and suspense.

Ming Vase:

The vase has no back, and Lettie escapes through a hole in the wall behind it. Before the vase is carried off, the prop man closes a trap door in the wall from behind, so that the wall looks intact when the vase is gone.

Flint's Death:

Another flash powder "bomb," located in a can Offstage of the kitchen door accomplishes this, augmented by a taped explosion through a speaker Stage Left, and a prop man giving the swinging door a quick push Onstage. A CO_2 cannister is aimed from Offstage through the door. When it swings open it will give the effect of leaking gas . . . use for just a moment.

Tweed's Death:

Located Stage Left on the wall above the desk is the mount for the four spears used in "Carry On." A fifth spear, in the middle, remains. The head of this "spear" is split down the middle into "jaws," one of which is pivoted and moveable. The body of the spear extends through the wall to backstage where a prop man operates the jaw by means of a control rod through the hollow spear. He can also move the spear up and down, side to side, and twist, as the spear rides in a pivoted sleeve mounted in the wall. A scrimmed hole in the wall is necessary so the operator can see to manipulate the spear to grab Tweed's muffler.

Gramophone:

The portrait of Lord Rancour above the mantel Stage Right is in fact a door which is hinged Upstage. On the back of this door is mounted a shelf on which the Gramophone rests. On cue, the prop man pushes the door open, and it swings Onstage, revealing the Gramophone.

PROPERTY LIST

18 toy telephones
4 kerosene storm lamps
1 knapsack
1 shirt
1 pair pants
1 oval tray with cup and saucer
1 tanqueray bottle
4 gin glasses
1 vase 10" x 4" with 2 dozen carnations
1 rectangular tray 10" x 14"
4 brand snifters 6"
1 brandy decanter
1 brass candlestick with candle
1 chrome serving tray 16" diameter with scalloped edge
1 sherry decanter
12 sherry glasses
1 rectangular chrome serving tray with handles 12" x 18"
1 whisky decanter
1 glass ashtray 3" diameter
1 trick decanter, stopper for will
1 toy pistol
1 working blank pistol—.22
1 trick phone on pallette
waste basket for Flint's bomb
claw spear
4 spears
3 dust covers
C-clamp for pouffe
head and fern for pouffe
1 large wicker
4 rain slickers with hats
1 easel
1 wicker cat carrier
2 matching wicker valises
1 brown leather suitcase
1 brown suede bag with parasol
1 hat box buff/orange
1 golf bag with 7 woods
1 shotgun
1 feather duster
1 small brown valise
2 mats
1 shoe
1 pallet and brush
1 ming vase 4'
1 brandy table

1 hearth broom—dressing
1 fireplace set—dressing, with brush, shovel, poker (working prop)
1 fire screen
2 candlesticks with candles—dressing
1 brass urn—dressing
1 elk head—dressing
2 velvet spears 6'—dressing
1 sword in sheath—dressing
1 portrait in frame with light (portrait of Lord Dudley Rancour)
1 victrola
9 lamp shades
1 4' x 6' Persian rug
1 8" x 8" plexi square for strobe in floor
1 drinks table 18" x 3'
1 plain torchiere
1 trick torchiere
1 swivel chair
1 doctor's bag
1 stethescope
1 smelling salts
1 toy gun
1 garden shears
1 cut telephone
2 marble bookends—dressing
1 letter box/letters—dressing
1 pen in stand—dressing
1 6" urn—dressing
1 letter box with letters—dressing
2 poison darts
1 large candle with stand—dressing
1 blotter (large)—dressing
1 hand blotter—dressing
3 dozen books—dressing
2 wooden swords—dressing
1 spear holder
1 powder horn—dressing
1 shield—dressing
1 axe—dressing
1 breast plate—dressing
1 helmet with plume—dressing
drum for stair bomb
drape with fringe—dressing
1 black upholstered chair—dressing
1 grandfather clock—dressing
draperies with traverse rod
1 gold upholstered chair—dressing
2 framed prints 10" x 14"—dressing
1 watercolor 16" x 24"—dressing
1 chamber pot
4 mirrors Offstage (for quick changes)
2 chandeliers

stationery
wills
1 tape measure

Running Needs:
Robert Burns Cigarellos
kitchen matches
bread
solicitor notes
iced tea mix
.22 cal. blanks
calling cards

Personal Props:
2 pocket watches—(Colonel, Tweed)
cigarette holder—(Nigel)
small note pad—(Tweed)
retracting pencil—(Tweed)
pipe—(Flint)

SHOW CUES—PROPS

ACT ONE:
    Hand rectangular tray at kitchen door at car horn.

    Receive props Upstage Center (Right and Left) from butler.

    Set Doctor's bag (open) Stage Left of small door in Upstage hallway downstairs

    Number 1 explosion (barrel under stairs—cover barrel right away)

    Gas telephone—pushed out and gas blown in tube. Pull telephone back and close door fast.

INTERMISSION

    Reset:

    1. Reset palette and brush from Upstairs Right to downstairs hall Stage Right near the easel.

    2. Set small rug at Downstage Right door on stage.

    3. Pick up cigar.

    4. Strike real gun lock up.

    5. Untie easel—candle to mantel and spear.

ACT TWO:
    Operate sconce on landing of stairway at end of first song.

    Operate pouffe.

    Open door in back of Ming vase and set crash mattresses.

    Catch actress at back of vase and throw shoe after belch. Remove mattresses and put in rug and lower and secure door.

    Number 2 explosion. Fan smoke out of kitchen.

    At end of song hand easel (untied) and palette to actress at hall Stage Right.

    Claw spear

    1. *Good grip* on scarf

    2. Have *red markings* on spear up

    3. Pull *up* and *back.*

    4. Secure spear.

    Gramophone—Stage Right.

Personal Requirements:

Cast:

    4 women

    6 men

Understudies:

    a woman to cover Tweed and Lady Manley-Prowe

    a woman to cover Hope and Lettie

    a man to cover Geoffrey, Nigel, and Clive

    a man to cover Flint, Dr. Grayburn, Colonel Gillweather

    total: 4 understudies

Musicians:

    trombone

    banjo

    trumpet
    bass
    reed 1
    reed 2
    percussion 1 & 2
    total: 8 musicians
Staff:
    stage manager
      assistant stage Manager
    electrician
    follow spot operator
    prop person
    sound person
    wardrobe person
Total Personal: 29

FAVORITE MUSICALS *from* "The House of Plays"

PHANTOM

(All Groups) Book by Arthur Kopit. Music & Lyrics by Maury Yeston. Large cast of m. & f. roles—doubling possible. Various Ints. & Exts. This sensational new version of Gaston Leroux' *The Phantom of the Opera* by the team which gave you *Nine* wowed audiences and critics alike with its beautiful music and lyrics, and expertly crafted book, which gives us more background information on beautiful Christine Daee and the mysterious Erik than even the original novel does. Christine is here an untrained street singer discovered by Count Philippe de Chandon, champagne tycoon. Erik, the Phantom of the Opera, is the illegitimate son of a dancer and the opera's manager. He becomes obsessed with the lovely Christine because her voice reminds him of his dead mother's. "Reminiscent of *The Hunchback of Notre Dame, Cyrano de Bergerac* and *The Elephant Man, Phantom*'s love story—and the passionately soaring music it prompts—are deliciously sentimental. Add Erik's father lovingly acknowledging his parenthood as his son is dying and the show jerks enough tears to fill that Paris Opera Lagoon."—San Diego Union. "Yeston and Kopit get us to care about the characters by telling us a lot about them, some of it funny, but most of it poignant."—Houston Chronicle. **(#18958)**

FAVORITE MUSICALS *from*

"The House of Plays"

A FINE AND PRIVATE PLACE

(**All Groups**) Book & Lyrics by Erik Haagensen. Music by Richard Isen. Adapted from the novel by Peter S. Beagle. 3m., 2f, (may be played by 2m., 2f.) + 1 raven (may be either m. or f.) Ext. setting. "The grave's a fine and private place,/But none, I think, do there embrace." Little did you know, Andrew Marvell, that someday, someone would come up with a charming love story, set in a graveyard, about two lost souls who are buried there, who meet and fall in love. Also inhabiting the cemetery is an eccentric old man who has the gift of being able to see and converse with the inhabitants of the graves, as well as with a raven who swoops in at mealtimes with some dinner he has swiped for the old guy. Also present from time to time is a delightful old Jewish widow, whose husband Morris is buried in the cemetery. She often stops by to tell Morris what's new. Her name is Gertrude, and it is soon apparent that she also stops by to flirt with old Jonathan Rebeck (she doesn't know he actually *lives* there). A crisis arises when it appears the young couple will be separated. The young man, it seems, has been deemed a suicide and, as such, he must be removed from consecrated ground. Their only hope is Jonathan; but to help them Jonathan must come out in the open. Had we but world enough, and time, we would tell you how Jonathan manages to salvage the romance; but we'll just have to hope the above story intrigues you enough to examine the delightful libretto and wonderfully tuneful music for yourself. A sell-out, smash hit at the Goodspeed in Connecticut and, later, at the American Stage Co. in New Jersey (the professional theatre which premiered *Other People's Money*), this happy, whimsical, sentimental, up-beat new show will delight audiences of all ages. . (**#8154**)

Other Publications for Your Interest

MAIL
(ADVANCED GROUPS—MUSICAL)
Book & Lyrics by JERRY COLKER
Music by MICHAEL RUPERS

9 men, 6 women—2 Sets

What a terrific idea for a "concept musical"! As *Mail* opens Alex, an unpublished novelist, is having an acute anxiety attack over his lack of success in writing and his indecision regarding his girlfriend, Dana; so, he "hits the ground running" and doesn't come back for 4 months! When Alex finally returns to his apartment, he finds an unending stream of messages on his answering machine and stacks and stacks of unopened mail. As he opens his mail, it in effect comes to life, as we learn what has been happening with Alex's friends, and with Dana, during his absence. There is also some hilarious junk mail, which bombards Alex muscially, as well as unpaid bills from the likes of the electric company (the ensemble comes dancing out of Alex's refrigerator singing "We're Gonna Turn Off Your Juice"). In the second act, we move into a sort of abstract vision of Alex's world, a blank piece of paper upon which he can, if he is able, and if he wishes, start over—with his writing, with his friends, with his father and, maybe, with Dana. Producers looking for something wild and crazy will, we know, want to open *this* MAIL, a hit with audiences and critics coast-to-coast, from the authors of THREE GUYS NAKED FROM THE WAIST DOWN! "At least 12 songs are solid enough to stand on their own. If MAIL can't deliver, there is little hope for the future of the musical theatre, unless we continue to rely on the British to take possession of a truly American art form."—Drama-Logue. "Make room for the theatre's newest musical geniuses."—The Same. (Terms quoted on application. Music available on rental. See p. 48.)

(#15199)

CHESS
(ADVANCED GROUPS—MUSICAL/OPERA)
Book by RICHARD NELSON
Lyrics by TIM RICE
Music by BJORN ULVAEUS & BENNY ANDERSSON

9 men, 2 women, 1 female child, plus ensemble

A *musical* about an *international chess match*?!?! A bad idea from the get-go, you'd think; but no—Tim Rice (he of *Evita, Joseph and the Amazing Technicolor Dreamcoat* and *Jesus Christ Superstar*), Bjorn Ulvaeus and Benny Andersson (they of Swedish Supergroup ABBA) and noted American playwright Richard Nelson, all in collaboration with Trevor Nunn (*Les Miz., Nick Nick*, etc.) have pulled it off, creating an extraordinary rock opera about international intrigue which uses as a metaphor a media-drenched chess match between a loutish American champion (shades of Bobby Fischer) and a nice-guy Soviet champion. The American has a girlfriend, Florence, there in Bangkok (where the match takes place) to be his second and to provide moral support. There she meets, and falls in love with, Anatoly, the Soviet champion—and the sparks fly, particularly when Anatoly decides to defect to the west, causing a postponement and change of venue to Budapest. Eventually, it is clear that all the characters are merely pawns in a larger chess match between the C.I.A. and the KGB! The pivotal role of Florence is perhaps the most extra-ordinary and complex role in the musical theatre since Eva Peron; and the roles of Freddie and Anatoly (both tenors) are great, too. Several of the songs have become international hits, including Florence's "Heaven Help My Heart", "I know Him So Well" and "Nobody's On Nobody's Side", and Freddie's descent into the maelstrom of decadence, "One Night in Bangkok". Playing to full houses and standing ovations, *Chess* closed exceedingly prematurely on Broadway; and, perhaps the story behind *that* just might make the basis of another Rice/ABBA/Nelson/Nunn collaboration! (Terms quoted on application. Music available on rental. See p. 48.) Slightly restricted.

(#5236)

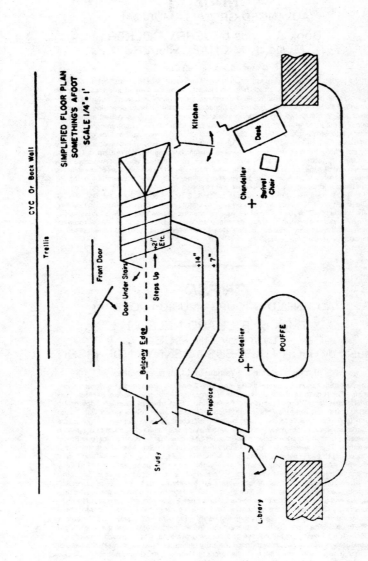

CYC Or Back Wall

Trellis

SIMPLIFIED FLOOR PLAN
SOMETHING'S AFOOT
SCALE 1/4" = 1'

Front Door

Door Under Stairs

Balcony Edge

Steps Up → +21"
Etc.

+14"

+7"

Study

Fireplace

Chandelier

+

POUFFE

Library

Kitchen

Desk

Chandelier

+

Swivel
Chair